Colette, the creator of Claudine, Chéri and Gigi, and one of France's outstanding writers, had a long, varied and active life. She was born in Burgundy in 1873, into a home overflowing with dogs, cats and children, and educated at the local village school. At the age of twenty she was brought to Paris by her first husband, the notorious Henry Gauthiers-Villars (Willy), writer and critic. By dint of locking her in her room, Willy forced Colette to write her first novels (the Claudine sequence), which he published under his name. They were an instant success. But their marriage (chronicled in *Mes Apprentissages)* was never happy and Colette left him in 1906. She spent the next six years on the stage - an experience, like that of her early childhood, which would provide many of the themes for her work. She remarried (*Julie de Carneilhan* 'is a close a reckoning with the elements of her second marriage as she ever allowed herself'), later divorcing her second husband, with whom she had a daughter. In 1935 she married Maurice Goudeket, with whom she lived until her death in 1954.

With the publication of *Chéri* (1920) Colette's place as one of France's prose masters became assured. Although she became increasingly crippled with arthritis, she never lost her intense preoccupation with everything around her. 'I cannot interest myself in anything that is not life,' she said; and, to a young writer, 'Look for a long time at what pleases you, and longer still at what pains you'. Her rich and supple prose, with its sensuous detail and sharp psychological insights, illustrates that personal philosophy.

Her writing runs to fifteen volumes, novels, portraits, essays, *chroniques* and a large body of autobiographical prose. She was the first woman President of the Académie Goncourt, and when she died was given a state funeral and buried in Père-Lachaise cemetery in Paris.

ALSO BY COLETTE

Fiction

Claudine and Annie
Claudine Married
Claudine in Paris
The Last of Chéri
Gigi and *The Cat*
Chance Acquaintances
Julie de Carneilhan
The Ripening Seed
The Vagabond
Break of Day
The Innocent Libertine
Mitsou
The Other One
The Shackle

Non-Fiction

My Apprenticeships and *Music-Hall Sidelights*
The Blue Lantern
My Mother's House and *Sido*
The Pure and the Impure

Colette

CHÉRI

TRANSLATED BY
Roger Senhouse

VINTAGE

Published by Vintage 2001

10

Copyright © Estate of Colette, 1920

Chéri first published by Fayard, Paris, 1920
First English translation published by Gollancz, 1930
This translation published by
Martin Secker & Warburg, 1951

Vintage
Random House, 20 Vauxhall Bridge Road,
London SW1V 2SA

www.vintage-books.co.uk

Addresses for companies within The Random House Group Limited
can be found at: www.randomhouse.co.uk/offices.htm

The Random House Group Limited Reg. No. 954009

A CIP catalogue record for this book
is available from the British Library

ISBN 9780099422761

The Random House Group Limited supports The Forest Stewardship
Council (FSC), the leading international forest certification organisation.
All our titles that are printed on Greenpeace approved FSC certified paper
carry the FSC logo. Our paper procurement policy can be found at:
www.rbooks.co.uk/environment

Printed and bound in Great Britain by
CPI Cox & Wyman, Reading, RG1 8EX

'GIVE it me, Léa, give me your pearl necklace! Do you hear me, Léa? Give me your pearls!'

No answer came from the huge brass-bedecked wrought-iron bedstead that glimmered in the shadows like a coat of mail.

'Why won't you let me have your necklace? It looks every bit as well on me as on you – even better!'

At the snap of the clasp, ripples spread over the lace-frilled sheets, and from their midst rose two magnificent thin-wristed arms, lifting on high two lovely lazy hands.

'Leave it alone, Chéri! You've been playing long enough with that necklace.'

'It amuses me. ... Are you frightened I'll steal it?'

He was capering about in front of the sun-drenched rosy-pink curtains – a graceful demon, black against a glowing furnace; but when he pranced back towards the bed, he turned white again from top to toe, in his white silk pyjamas and white Moorish slippers.

'I'm not frightened,' the soft, deep voice answered from the bed. 'But you'll wear out the thread. Those pearls are heavy.'

'They certainly are,' Chéri said with due respect. 'Whoever gave you this lot never meant to make light of you!'

He was standing in front of a pier-glass framed in the space between two windows, gazing at the reflection of a very youthful, very good-looking young man, neither too short nor too tall, hair with the blue sheen of a blackbird's plumage. He unbuttoned his pyjamas, displaying a hard, darkish chest, curved like a shield; and the whites of his dark eyes, his teeth, and the pearls of the necklace gleamed in the over-all rosy glow of the room.

'Take off that necklace!' The female voice was insistent. 'Do you hear what I say?'

The young man, motionless in front of his image, laughed softly to himself: 'Yes, yes, I heard you. I know so well you're terrified I'll make off with it!'

'No, I'm not. But if I did offer it to you, you're quite capable of taking it.'

I

He ran to the bed and bounded into it. 'You bet I am! I rise above the conventions. Personally, I think it's idiotic for a man to allow a woman to give him a single pearl for a tie-pin, or two for a pair of studs, and then to consider himself beyond the pale if she gives him fifty. ...'

'Forty-nine.'

'Forty-nine – as if I hadn't counted! I dare you to say they don't look well on me! Or that I'm ugly!'

Léa sat up in bed. 'No, I won't say that. For one thing, because you'd never believe me. But can't you learn to laugh without crinkling up your nose like that? I suppose you won't be happy till you've wrinkles all up the side of your nose!'

He stopped laughing at once, let the skin on his forehead relax, and drew in the fold under his chin like a coquettish old woman. They looked at each other in open hostility – she, leaning on her elbow in a flurry of frills and lace; he, sitting side-saddle on the edge of the bed. He was thinking 'Who's she to talk of any wrinkles I may have one day?' and she 'Why is he so ugly when he laughs? – he who's the very picture of beauty!' She thought for a moment, then finished aloud: 'It's because you look so ill-natured when you're joking. You never laugh except unkindly – *at* people, and that makes you ugly. You're often ugly.'

'That's not true!' Chéri exclaimed crossly.

Anger knitted his eyebrows close above his nose, magnified his eyes, glittering with insolence behind a palisade of lashes, and parted the chaste bow of his disdainful mouth. Léa smiled to see him as she loved him best: rebellious only to become submissive, enchained lightly but powerless to free himself. She put a hand on his young head, which impatiently shook off the yoke. Like someone quieting an animal, she murmured, 'There, there! What is it? What is it, then?'

He fell upon her big beautiful shoulder, nuzzling and butting his way into his favourite resting-place with eyes already shut, seeking his customary long morning sleep in the protection of her arms. But Léa pushed him away. 'None of that now, Chéri! You're having luncheon with our national Harpy, and it's already twenty to twelve!'

2

'Not really? I'm lunching at the old girl's? You too?'

Lazily Léa settled deeper into the bed.

'Not me, I'm off duty. I'll go for coffee at half past two, or tea at six, or for a cigarette at a quarter to eight. Don't worry; she'll always see enough of me. And besides, I've not been asked.'

Chéri's sulky face lit up with malice.

'I know, I know why! We're going to have high society. We're going to have the fair Marie-Laure, and that poisonous child of hers.'

Léa brought her big blue wandering eyes to rest.

'Oh, really! The little girl's charming. Less so than her mother, but charming. Now take off that necklace, once and for all.'

'Pity,' Chéri sighed, as he undid the clasp. 'It would look so well in the trousseau.'

Léa raised herself on her elbow: 'What trousseau?'

'Mine,' Chéri said with ludicrous self-importance. '*My* trousseau, full of *my* jewels, for *my* marriage!'

He bounded in the air, executed a perfect *entrechat-six*, returned to earth, butted his way through the door-curtains, and disappeared, shouting: 'My bath, Rose! And quick about it! I'm lunching at the old girl's!'

'That's that,' Léa thought. 'We'll have a lake in the bathroom and eight towels floating in it, and razor scrapings in the basin. If only I had two bathrooms!'

But, as on former occasions, she soon saw that this would mean getting rid of a wardrobe and lopping off a corner of her dressing-room, and so concluded, as on former occasions: 'I shall simply have to put up with it till Chéri gets married.'

She lay down again on her back and noticed that Chéri, undressing the night before, had thrown his socks on the mantelpiece, his pants on the writing-table, his tie round the neck of her portrait bust. She could not help smiling at this hasty masculine disorder, and half closed her large tranquil eyes. Their blue was as beautiful as ever, and so were the thick chestnut lashes.

At the age of forty-nine, Léonie Vallon, called Léa de Lonval, was nearing the end of a successful career as a richly kept courtesan. She was a good creature, and life had spared her the more flattering catastrophes and exalted sufferings. She made a secret of the date of her birth; but willingly admitted – with a look of voluptuous condescension for Chéri's special benefit – that she was approaching the age when she could indulge in a few creature comforts. She liked order, fine linen, wines in their prime, and carefully planned meals at home. From an idolized young blonde she had become a rich middle-aged *demi-mondaine* without ever attracting any outrageous publicity. Not that she went in for any pretences. Her friends remembered a Four-in-Hand Meet at Auteuil, about 1895, when the subeditor of *Gil Blas* had addressed her as 'dear artist' and she had answered: 'Artist! Oh come, my good friend, my lovers must have been telling tales. ...'

Her contemporaries were jealous of her imperturbable good health, and the younger women, whose figures were padded out in front and behind after the fashion of 1912, scoffed at her opulent bust. Young and old alike envied her the possession of Chéri.

'Though, good heavens!' Léa used to say, 'there's no reason why they should. They're welcome to him! I don't keep him on a lead. He goes out by himself.'

But in this she was not altogether speaking the truth, for she was proud of a liaison – sometimes, in her weakness for the truth, referring to it as 'an adoption' – that had lasted six years.

'Trousseau,' Léa said over again. 'Marriage for Chéri! It's not possible, it's not ... human ... you can't give an innocent girl to Chéri! Why, it would be throwing a doe to the hounds! People don't know what Chéri is!'

As if telling the beads of a rosary, she ran her fingers over the necklace which Chéri had tossed on the bed. She put it away at night now because, with his passion for fine pearls and his fondness for playing with them in the morning, he would have noticed too often that her throat had thickened and was not nearly so white, with the muscles under its skin growing slack. She fastened the pearls round her neck without getting up, and took a hand-mirror from the bedside-table.

'I look like a gardener's wife,' was her unflattering comment, 'a market-gardener's wife. A market-gardener's wife in Normandy, off to the potato-fields wearing a pearl necklace. I might as well stick an ostrich feather in my nose – and that's being polite!'

She shrugged her shoulders, severely critical of everything she no longer loved in herself: the vivid complexion, healthy, a little too ruddy – an open-air complexion, well suited to emphasize the pure intensity of her eyes, with their varying shades of blue. Her proud nose still won her approval. 'Marie-Antoinette's nose!' Chéri's mother was in the habit of saying, without ever forgetting to add: 'and in another two years our Léa will have a chin like Louis Seize.' Her mouth, with its even row of teeth, seldom opened in a peal of laughter; but she smiled often, a smile that set off to perfection the lazy flutter of her large eyes – a smile a hundred times lauded, sung, and photographed – a deep, confiding smile one never tired of watching.

As for her body – 'Everyone knows', Léa would say, 'that a well-made body lasts a long time.' She could still afford to show her body, pink and white, endowed with the long legs and straight back of a naiad on an Italian fountain; the dimpled hips, the high-slung breasts, 'would last', Léa used to say, 'till well after Chéri's wedding.'

She got out of bed, and, slipping into a wrap, went to draw back the long curtains. The noonday sun poured into the gay, rosy, over-decorated room. Its luxury dated: double lace curtains, rose-bud watered silk on the walls, gilded woodwork, and antique furniture upholstered in modern silks. Léa refused to give up either this cosy room or its bed, a massive and indestructible masterpiece of wrought iron and brass, grim to the eye and cruel to the shins.

'Come, come!' Chéri's mother protested, 'it's not as bad as all that. Personally, I like this room. It belongs to a period. It has a style of its own. It suggests La Païva.'

The remembrance of this dig made Léa smile as she pinned up her hair. She hurriedly powdered her face on hearing two doors slam, and the thud of a male foot colliding with some delicate piece of furniture. Chéri came back into the room in shirt and trousers, his ears white with talcum powder. He was in an aggressive mood.

'Where's my tie-pin? What a wretched hole this is! Have they taken to pinching the jewellery?'

'Marcel must have stuck it in his tie to go to the market,' Léa gravely replied.

Chéri, who had little or no sense of humour, was brought up short by the little quip like an ant by a lump of coal. He stopped his angry pacing up and down, and found nothing better to say than: 'Charming! and what about my boots?'

'Your what?'

'The calf, of course!'

Léa smiled up at him from her dressing-table, too affectionately. 'You said it, not I,' she murmured in caressing tones.

'The day when a woman loves me for my brains,' he retorted, 'I shall be done for. Meanwhile I must have my pin and my boots.'

'What for? You don't wear a tie-pin with a lounge suit, and you've got one pair on already.'

Chéri stamped his foot. 'I've had enough of this! There's nobody here to look after me, and I'm sick of it all.'

Léa put down her comb. 'Very well, say goodbye to it all for good!'

He shrugged his shoulders, like a young tough. 'You wouldn't like it if I did!'

'Be off with you! I hate guests who complain of the cooking and leave bits and pieces all over the place and cream-cheese sticking to the mirrors. Go back to your sainted mother, my child, and stay there.'

Unable to meet Léa's gaze, he lowered his eyes, and broke out into schoolboy protests. 'Soon I shan't be allowed to open my mouth! Anyhow, you'll let me have your motor to go to Neuilly?'

'No.'

'Why not?'

'Because I'm going out in it myself at two, and because the chauffeur is having his dinner.'

'Where are you going at two?'

'To say my prayers. But if you need three francs for a taxi ... Idiot,' she added tenderly. 'At two I'll probably come to your lady mother's for coffee. Does that satisfy you?'

He tossed his head like a young buck. 'You bite my head off, you won't give me anything I ask for; they hide my things away, they—'

'Will you never learn to dress yourself?'

She took the tie from Chéri's hands and tied it for him.

'There! And that frightful purple tie. ... However, it's just the thing for the fair Marie-Laure and family. ... And you wanted to wear a pearl on top of all that! You little dago. .... Why not earrings into the bargain?'

His defences were down. Blissful, languid, irresolute, supine, he surrendered again to a lazy happiness and closed his eyes. ...

'Nounoune darling ...' he murmured.

She brushed the hair off his ears, combed a straighter parting in the bluish locks of his black hair, dabbed a little scent on his temples, and gave him a quick kiss, unable to resist the tempting mouth so close to her own.

Chéri opened his eyes, and his lips, then stretched out his hands.

She moved away. 'No. It's a quarter to one! Be off now, and don't let me see you again!'

'Never?'

'Never,' she laughed back at him with uncontrollable tenderness.

Left to herself, she smiled proudly, and a sharp little sigh of defeated desire escaped her as she listened to Chéri's footsteps crossing the courtyard. She saw him open and close the gates, drift away on his winged feet, only to encounter the adoring glances of three shop girls walking along arm-in-arm.

'Lawks! He's too good to be true! Let's touch him to see if he's real!'

But Chéri took it all for granted and did not even turn round.

'M Y bath, Rose! Tell the manicurist she can go, it's far too late now. My blue coat and skirt – the new one – the blue hat with the white under-brim, and the little shoes with the straps ... No, wait ...'

Léa, with one leg across the other, rubbed her ankle and shook her head.

'No, the blue kid laced boots. My legs are a little swollen today. It's the heat.'

Her elderly maid, butterfly-capped, raised understanding eyes to Léa. 'It's ... it's the heat,' she repeated obediently, shrugging her shoulders as much as to say: 'We know ... Nothing lasts for ever. ...'

With Chéri out of the house, Léa became herself again, very much alive, cheerful, and on the spot. Within an hour, she had been given her bath, followed by a spirit-rub scented with sandal-wood, and was ready dressed, hatted, and shod. While the curling-tongs were heating, she found time to run through the butler's book and send for Émile, the footman, and call his attention to the blue haze on one of the looking-glasses. She ran an experienced eye – rarely taken in – over everything in the room, and lunched in solitary bliss, with a smile for the dry Vouvray and for the June strawberries, served, with their stalks, on a plate of Rubelles enamel as green as a tree-frog after rain. Someone in the past who appreciated good food must have chosen the huge Louis Seize looking-glasses and the English furniture of the same period for this rectangular dining-room, light, airy sideboards, high pedestalled dumb-waiters, spindly yet strong Sheraton chairs, in a dark wood with delicate swags. The looking-glasses and the massive silver caught the full light of day, with a touch of green reflected from the trees in the Avenue Bugeaud. Léa, as she ate, examined a fork for any suspicion of pink cleaning-powder left in the chasing, and half closed one eye the better to judge the quality of the polish on the dark wood. Standing behind her, the butler watched this performance nervously.

'Marcel!' Léa said, 'for the last week or so, the wax on your floors has been smeary.'

8

'Does Madame think so?'

'Madame does think so. Add a little turpentine while you're melting it in a double saucepan; it's quite easy to do again. You brought up the Vouvray a little too soon. Close the shutters as soon as you've cleared the table; we're in for a heat-wave.'

'Very good, Madame. Will Monsieur Ch – Monsieur Peloux be dining?'

'Probably. ... No *crème-surprise* tonight. We'll just have a strawberry water ice. Coffee in the boudoir.'

As she rose from the table, straight and tall, the shape of her legs visible under a dress that moulded her hips, she had ample time to note the 'Madame is beautiful' in the butler's discreet glance, and this did not displease her.

'Beautiful,' Léa whispered on her way up to the boudoir. 'No. ... No longer. I have now to wear something white near my face, and very pale pink underclothes and tea-gowns. Beautiful! Pish. ... I hardly need to be that any longer.'

All the same, she allowed herself no siesta in the painted silk boudoir, when she had finished with coffee and the newspapers. And it was with battle written on her face that she gave her chauffeur the order: 'To Madame Peloux's.'

The tree-lined road through the Bois, dry beneath the young, already arid, faded June foliage – the toll-gate – Neuilly – Boulevard d'Inkermann – 'How many times have I come this way?' Léa wondered. She began to count, then tired of counting and softened her tread on the gravel outside Madame Peloux's house to overhear any sounds coming from it.

'They're in the garden-room,' she concluded.

She had put on more powder before approaching the house and tightened the fine-mesh, misty blue veil under her chin. Her answer to the manservant's formal request to come through the house was: 'No; I'd rather go round by the garden.'

A real garden – almost a park – completely surrounded the vast white villa, typical of the outer suburbs of Paris. Madame Peloux's villa had been called 'a country residence' in the days when Neuilly was still on the outskirts of Paris. This was apparent from the stables, converted into garages, the other offices with their kennels and wash-houses, not to mention the size of the billiard-room, entrance hall, and dining-room.

'This is a handsome investment of Madame Peloux's,' her female devotees never tired of repeating – the old toadies who, in exchange for a dinner or a glass of brandy, came there to take a hand against her at bezique or poker. And they added: 'But then, where has Madame Peloux not got money invested?'

Walking along in the shade of the acacia trees, between trellised roses and huge clumps of rhododendrons in full blaze, Léa could hear the murmur of voices, and, rising above it, Madame Peloux's shrill nasal trumpet notes and Chéri's dry cackle.

'That child's got an ugly laugh,' she thought. She paused a moment to listen more attentively to a new feminine note; weak, pleasing, quickly drowned by the redoubtable trumpeting. 'That must be the girl,' she said to herself, and a few quick steps brought her to the garden-room with its glass front, from which Madame Peloux burst out with a 'Here comes our beautiful friend!'

A little round barrel of a woman, Madame Peloux – in reality Mademoiselle Peloux – had been a ballet-dancer from her tenth to her sixteenth year. Occasionally Léa would search for some trace in Madame Peloux that might recall the once chubby little fair-haired Eros, or the later dimpled nymph, and found nothing except the big implacable eyes, the delicate aggressive nose, and a still coquettish way of standing with her feet in 'the fifth position', like the members of the *corps de ballet*.

Chéri, coming to life in the depths of a rocking-chair, kissed Léa's hand with involuntary grace and ruined his gesture by ex-claiming: 'Hang it all! you've put on a veil again, and I loathe veils.'

'Will you leave her alone!' Madame Peloux interposed. 'You must never ask a woman why she is wearing a veil. We'll never be able to do anything with him,' she said to Léa affectionately.

Two women had risen to their feet in the golden shade of a straw blind. One, in mauve, rather coldly offered her hand to Léa, who looked her over from head to foot.

'Goodness, how lovely you are, Marie-Laure! you're perfection itself!'

Marie-Laure deigned to smile. She was a red-haired young woman with brown eyes, whose physical presence alone was enough to take your breath away. She drew attention, almost coquettishly, to the other young woman, by saying: 'But would you have recognized my daughter Edmée?'

Léa held out a hand which the girl was reluctant to shake.

'I should have known you, my child, but a schoolgirl alters so quickly, and Marie-Laure alters only to become always more disconcertingly lovely. Are you quite finished with school now?'

'I should hope so, I should hope so,' exclaimed Madame Peloux. 'You can't go on for ever, hiding her under a bushel, such a miracle of grace and charm, and she's nineteen already!'

'Eighteen,' said Marie-Laure sweetly.

'Eighteen, eighteen! ... Yes of course, eighteen! Léa, you remember? This child was just making her first Communion the year that Chéri ran away from school, surely you remember? Yes, yes, you did, you little good-for-nothing, you ran away and Léa and I were driven nearly out of our wits!'

'I remember perfectly,' Léa said, and she exchanged an imperceptible little nod with Marie-Laure – something corresponding to the '*touché*' of a punctilious fencer.

'You must get her married soon, you must get her married soon!' pursued Madame Peloux, who never failed to repeat a basic truth at least twice. 'We'll all come to the wedding.'

She brandished her little arms in the air, and the young girl glanced at her with ingenuous alarm.

'She's just the daughter for Marie-Laure,' thought Léa, gazing at her more closely. 'She has all her mother's dazzling qualities but in a quieter key: fluffy, ash-brown hair, that looks as if it were powdered; frightened, secretive eyes and a mouth she avoids opening even to speak or smile. ... Exactly what Marie-Laure needs as a foil – but how she must hate her!'

Madame Peloux insinuated a maternal smile between Léa and the young girl: 'You ought to have seen how well these two young people were getting on together in the garden!'

She pointed to where Chéri stood smoking a cigarette on the other side of the glass partition, his cigarette-holder clenched between his teeth, and his head tilted back to avoid the smoke. The three women looked at the young man who – forehead held at an angle, eyes half shut, feet together, motionless – looked for all the world like a winged figure hovering dreamily in the air. Léa did not fail to observe the expression of fright and subjugation in the girl's eyes, and she took pleasure in making her tremble by touching her on the arm. Edmée quivered from head to foot, withdrew her arm, and whispered almost savagely, 'What?'

'Nothing,' Léa replied, 'I dropped my glove.'

'Come along, Edmée!' Marie-Laure called negligently.

Silent and docile, the girl walked towards Madame Peloux, who flapped her wings: 'Leaving already? Surely not? We must meet again soon, we must meet again soon!'

'It's late,' Marie-Laure said, 'and you'll be expecting any number of people as it's Sunday afternoon. The child is not accustomed to company.'

'Of course not, of course not,' Madame Peloux said tenderly. 'She's had such a sheltered existence … such a lonely life!'

Marie-Laure smiled, and Léa gave her a look as much as to say, 'That's one for you!'

'But we'll call again soon.'

'Thursday, Thursday! Léa, you'll come to luncheon on Thursday?'

'I'll be here,' Léa answered.

Chéri had rejoined Edmée at the entrance to the room and stood beside her, disdaining all conversation. He had heard Léa's promise, and turned round: 'Splendid, then we can go for a run in the motor.'

'Yes, yes, just the thing for you young people,' Madame Peloux insisted, touched by his proposal. 'Edmée can sit in front next to Chéri, at the wheel, and the rest of us will go at the back. Youth at the helm, youth at the helm! Chéri, my love, will you ask for Marie-Laure's motor?'

Her small stumpy feet kept slipping on the gravel, but she managed to take her two visitors to the corner of the path, where she handed them over to Chéri. On her return, she found that Léa had taken off her hat and was smoking a cigarette.

'Aren't they sweet, those two!' Madame Peloux gasped. 'Don't you think so, Léa?'

'Delicious,' Léa breathed out in the same puff as her cigarette smoke. 'But really, that Marie-Laure!'

'What's Marie-Laure been up to?' asked Chéri, as he rejoined them.

'How lovely she is!'

'Ah! Ah!' Madame Peloux began in formal assent. 'That's true, that's true. She has been really lovely.'

Chéri and Léa caught each other's eye and laughed.

'Has been?' Léa emphasized the past tense. 'But she's the picture of youth. Not a single wrinkle! And she can wear the palest mauve, such a foul colour! I loathe it and it loathes me.'

Madame Peloux raised her big pitiless eyes and thin nose from her brandy-glass.

'The picture of youth, the picture of youth!' yapped Madame Peloux. 'Pardon me, pardon me! Marie-Laure had Edmée in 1895, no ... '94. She'd just run away with a singing-teacher, leaving Khalil Bey flat, though he'd given her the famous pink diamond which ... No, no! Wait! ... That must have been the year before!'

The trumpet notes were shrill and off key. Léa put a hand over her ear, and Chéri declared, with some feeling: 'Everything would be heavenly on an afternoon like this, if only we could be spared my mother's voice!'

She looked at her son with no sign of anger, accustomed to his insolence. Dignified, feet dangling, she settled herself back in a basket chair too high for her short legs. In one hand she warmed her glass of brandy. Léa, rocking herself gently to and fro, glanced occasionally at Chéri, who lay sprawled on a cool cane settee, coat unbuttoned, a cigarette dying between his lips, a lock of hair over one eyebrow. 'He's a handsome young blackguard,' she thought admiringly.

There they remained, peacefully side by side, making no effort to talk or be sociable, happy after their own fashion. Years of close familiarity rendered silence congenial and Chéri slipped back into his lethargy, Léa into her calm. As the afternoon became hotter, Madame Peloux pulled her narrow skirt up to her knees, displaying her tight little sailor's calves, and Chéri ripped off his tie – reproved by Léa in an audible 'Tch, tch'.

'Oh! leave the child alone,' Madame Peloux protested, as from the depths of a dream. 'It's much too hot! Would you care for a kimono, Léa?'

'No, thank you. I'm perfectly comfortable.'

Their unbuttoned siestas disgusted her. Never once had her young lover caught her untidily dressed, or with her blouse undone, or in her bedroom slippers during the day. 'Naked, if need be,' she would say, 'but squalid, never!'

She picked up her picture paper again, but did not read it. 'These Pelouxs – mother and son alike!' she thought dreamily. 'They've only to sit themselves down at a good meal or in the heart of the countryside and – snap! – the mother whisks off her stays and the son his waistcoat. They behave like publicans out on a holiday, the pair of them.' She cast a vindictive eye on one of the publicans in question, and saw that he had fallen asleep, his eyelashes spread against his pallid cheeks, his mouth closed. His upper lip, lit from below, reflected two silver pinpoints of light at the twin curves of its delicious Cupid's bow, and Léa was forced to admit that he looked far more like a sleeping god than a licensed victualler.

Without moving from her chair, she gently plucked the lighted cigarette from between Chéri's fingers and put it in the ash-tray. The hand of the sleeper relaxed and the tapering fingers, tipped with cruel nails, drooped like wilting flowers: a hand not strictly feminine, yet a trifle prettier than one could have wished; a hand she had kissed a hundred times – not in slavish devotion – but kissed for the pleasure of it, for its scent.

From behind her paper, she glanced at Madame Peloux. Was she asleep too? Léa always liked to remain awake while mother and son dozed, allowing her a quiet hour's self-communing in the dappled sunlight of a broiling afternoon. But Madame Peloux was not asleep. She was sitting bolt upright in her wickerwork chair, like a Buddha staring into space, and sipping her *fine-champagne* with the absorption of an alcoholic baby.

'Why doesn't she go to sleep?' Léa wondered. 'It's Sunday. She's lunched well. She's expecting her sponging old cronies to drop in for her five o'clock tea. By rights she ought to be having a snooze. If she's not snoozing, it's because she's up to some devilment or other.'

They had known each other for twenty-five years. Theirs was the hostile intimacy of light women, enriched and then cast aside by one man, ruined by another: the tetchy affection of rivals stalking one another's first wrinkle or white hair. Theirs was the friendship of two practical women of the world, both adepts at the money game; but one of them a miser, and the other a sybarite. These bonds count. Rather late in their day, a stronger bond had come to link them more closely: Chéri.

Léa could remember Chéri as a little boy – a marvel of beauty with long curls. When quite small he was known as Fred, and had not yet been nicknamed Chéri.

Sometimes forgotten and sometimes adored, Chéri grew up among wan housemaids and tall sardonic menservants. Although his birth had mysteriously brought wealth to the house, no 'Fräulein', no 'Miss' was ever to be seen at Chéri's side; and his mother had preserved him, to the accompaniment of piercing shrieks, from 'these ghouls'.

'Charlotte Peloux, you belong to another age.' The speaker was the moribund, mummified, but indestructible Baron de Berthellemy. 'Charlotte Peloux, in you I salute the only light woman who ever had the courage to bring up her son as the son of a tart! You belong to another age! You never read, you never travel, you make a point of knowing your neighbour's business, and you abandon your child to the tender mercies of the servants. How perfect! How absolutely About!* ... Or, better still, how like a novel by Gustav Droz. ... And to think that you've never heard of either! ...'

---

* Edmond About (*Roman d'un brave homme*, etc.) and Gustave Droz (*Monsieur, Madame et Bébé*, etc.), light popular novelists of the second half of the nineteenth century, some of whose books appeared in English translation, *Papa, Mamma and Baby*, illustrated by Morin 1887.

Chéri had enjoyed the full freedom of a profligate upbringing. When barely able to lisp, he was quick to pick up all the backstairs gossip. He shared in the clandestine suppers of the kitchen. His ablutions varied between milky immersions in his mother's orris-root baths and scanty cat-licks with the corner of a towel. He suffered from indigestion after a surfeit of sweets, or from pangs of hunger when no one remembered to give him his supper. He was wretchedly bored at every Battle of Flowers, where Charlotte Peloux would exhibit him – half-naked and catching cold – sitting on drenched roses; but it so happened, when he was twelve, that he had a glorious adventure in an illicit gambling-den, when an American woman allowed him to play with a fistful of louis d'or, and called him 'a little masterpiece'. At about the same time, Madame Peloux imposed a tutor on her son – an Abbé, whom she packed off at the end of ten months 'because', she confessed, 'whenever I caught sight of that black robe trailing along the passages, it made me think I was housing a female relation: and God knows there are few things more depressing than having a poor relation to stay!'

At the age of fourteen, Chéri had a taste of school. He didn't believe in it. He broke prison and ran away. Madame Peloux not only found the energy to incarcerate him a second time, but also, when faced with her son's tears and insults, took to her heels with hands over her ears screaming, 'I can't bear the sight of it! I can't bear the sight of it!' So sincere were her cries that she actually fled from Paris, in the company of a man who was young but far from scrupulous. Two years later she came back, alone. It was the last time she succumbed to an amorous impulse.

She found, on her return, that Chéri had shot up too fast; that his cheeks were hollow and his eyes black-ringed; that he dressed like a stable-lad and spoke with a worse accent than ever. She beat her breast, and snatched him back from the boarding-school. He utterly refused to work; demanded horses, carriages, jewels; insisted on a substantial monthly allowance; and, when his mother began to beat her breast and shriek like a pea-hen, he put a stop to her cries by saying: 'Madame Peloux, ma'am, don't carry on so. My venerable mother, if no one except me drags you down into the gutter, you're

likely to die a comfortable death in your downy bed; I don't altogether fancy a trustee for my estate. Your cash is mine. Let me go
my own way! Men friends cost next to nothing – a dinner and a bottle
of champagne. As for the fair sex, surely, Ma'me Peloux, seeing that
I take after you, you can trust me not to treat 'em to more than a
trinket – if that!'

He pirouetted about while she shed tears and proclaimed herself
the happiest of mothers. When Chéri began buying motor-cars, she
trembled once more; but he simply advised her: 'Keep an eye on the
petrol, Ma'me Peloux, if you please!' and sold his horses. He was
not above checking the two chauffeurs' books. His calculations were
quick and accurate, and the figures he jotted down on slips of paper –
dashed off rapidly, round and regular – were in marked contrast to
his rather slow and childish handwriting.

At seventeen he was like a little old man, always fussing over his
expenses: still good-looking – but skinny and short-winded. More
than once Madame Peloux ran into him on the cellar steps, coming up
from checking the bottles in the racks and bins.

'Would you believe it?' she said to Léa. 'It's too wonderful.'

'Much too wonderful,' Léa answered, 'he'll come to a bad end.
Chéri! Show me your tongue!'

He put out his tongue, made a face, and showed other signs
of disrespect. Léa took no notice. She was too intimate a friend,
a sort of doting godmother, whom he called by her Christian
name.

'Is it true', Léa inquired, 'that you were seen last night at a bar,
sitting on old Lili's knees?'

'Her knees!' scoffed Chéri. 'She hasn't had any for ages. They
foundered years ago.'

'Isn't it true', Léa persisted with greater severity, 'that she made
you drink gin laced with pepper? You know gin is bad for the
breath!'

On one occasion, Chéri, hurt, snapped back at Léa: 'I can't think
why you bother me with all these questions. You must have seen
what I was up to; you were tucked away in that cubby-hole at the
back, with Patron your prize-fighter friend.'

'That's perfectly correct,' Léa answered, unmoved. 'There's

nothing of the dissipated schoolboy about Patron. He has other attractions, and a good deal more to recommend him than a perky little face and two black rings round his eyes.'

That week Chéri had been out on the razzle in Montmartre and les Halles, consorting with ladies of the town who called him 'poppet' and 'my pet vice', but he had got no kick out of it: he suffered from migraines and a dry cough. Madame Peloux poured out her heart-breaking woes – 'Life is nothing but a series of crosses for us mothers' – to her masseuse, to her stay-maker, Madame Ribot, to old Lili, to the Baron de Berthellemy, and thus passed painlessly from the state of being the happiest-of-parents to that of the martyr-mother.

A night in June, when Madame Peloux and Léa and Chéri were together in the garden-room at Neuilly, was to change the destinies of the young man and the middle-aged woman. Chéri's friends had gone off for the evening – little Baxter, a wholesale wine-merchant, and the Vicomte Desmond, a hanger-on of his, barely of age, difficult and arrogant – and so Chéri had returned to the maternal fold, and habit had drawn Léa there also.

For one more evening, in a whole sequence of such occasions, these two women, each suspicious of the other, found themselves together. They had known each other for twenty years; they shared a past made up of similarly dull evenings; they lacked other friends; and, in their later days, they had become mistrustful, self-indulgent, and cut off from the world, as women are who have lived only for love.

Both were staring in silence at Chéri, who never spoke. Madame Peloux lacked the strength to take her son's health in hand, but hated Léa a little more each time she bent her white neck and glowing cheeks over Chéri's pallid cheek and transparent ear. She would willingly have bled that healthy female neck, already wrinkled by the so-called lines of Venus, in order to give a touch of colour to her slim lily-green son: yet it never occurred to her to take her darling away to the country.

'Chéri, why are you drinking brandy?' Léa scolded.

'Out of politeness to Ma'me Peloux – who would otherwise be drinking alone,' Chéri answered.

'What are you going to do tomorrow?'

'Dunno, and you?'

'I'm off to Normandy.'

'With?'

'That's none of your business.'

'With our friend Spéleïeff?'

'Don't be so stupid. That was over two months ago. You're behind the times. Spéleïeff's in Russia.'

'Chéri, darling, what can you be thinking of?' sighed Madame Peloux. 'Don't you remember going last month to the charming dinner given by Léa to celebrate the end of the affair? Léa, you've never let me have the recipe for those langoustines I enjoyed so much.'

Chéri sat up, his eyes sparkling. 'Yes, yes, langoustines, swimming in a creamy sauce! How I'd like some now!'

'You see,' Madame Peloux said reproachfully, 'he's got no appetite to speak of and yet he's asking for langoustines.'

'Shut up!' Chéri snapped. 'Léa, are you off to the shady woods with Patron?'

'Certainly not, my boy. Patron and I are merely friends. I'm going on my own.'

'Nice to be so rich!' Chéri threw out.

'I'll take you with me, if you like: there'll be nothing to do but eat and drink and sleep. ...'

'Where is this place of yours?' He had risen to his feet and was standing over her.

'You know Honfleur – the Côte de Grâce – don't you? Sit down; you're green in the face. Now as you go down the Côte de Grâce, you know those farm gates where we always say, in passing, your mother and I ...'

She turned round to where Madame Peloux was sitting. Madame Peloux had disappeared. The discretion with which she had faded away was something so unlike the normal Charlotte Peloux, that they looked at each other and laughed in surprise.

Chéri sat down close to Léa. 'I'm tired,' he said.

'You're ruining your health.'

He drew himself up in his chair, with offended vanity. 'Oh! I'm still in good enough fettle, you know.'

'Good enough! For others perhaps ... but not ... not for me, I'd have you know.'

'Too green?'

'The very word I was looking for. So why don't you come down to the country? No nonsense, of course. Ripe strawberries, fresh cream, cakes, grilled spring chicken ... that's just what you need – and no women.'

He let himself snuggle up to Léa's elbow and shut his eyes.

'No women ... grand ... Léa, tell me, you're my pal? You are? Then let's be off. Women indeed! I'm fed up with 'em. Women! I've seen all they've got to show.'

These vulgarities were muttered in a drowsy voice. Léa listened to his soft tone, and felt his warm breath against her ear. He had taken hold of her long string of pearls and was rolling the larger ones between his fingers. She slipped her arm under his head and so accustomed was she to treating the boy in this way that, almost without thinking, she pulled him towards her and rocked him in her arms.

'How comfy I am!' he sighed. 'You're a good pal. I'm so comfy.'

Léa smiled, as though hearing praise she valued intensely. Chéri seemed to be ready to drop off to sleep. She looked very closely at his glistening, almost dewy, eyelashes sunk flat against the cheeks, and then at the cheeks themselves, hollowed by his joyless dissipation. His upper lip, shaved that morning, was already bluish, and the pink lampshades lent his mouth an artificial colour.

'No women!' Chéri exclaimed, as though dreaming. 'Then ... kiss me!'

Taken by surprise, Léa made no movement.

'Kiss me! I tell you!'

He rapped out his order, frowning, and Léa felt embarrassed by the rekindled gleam in his eyes. It was as if someone had switched on the light. She shrugged her shoulders and kissed the forehead so close to her lips. He drew his arms tighter around her neck, and pulled her down towards him.

20

She shook her head only at the very instant that their lips touched, then she remained absolutely motionless, and held her breath like someone listening. When he released his hold, she broke away from him, rose to her feet, took a deep breath, and put a hand up to tidy her unruffled hair. She turned to him, rather pale and with rueful eyes, and said, teasingly: 'That was a bright idea!'

He lay far back in the rocking-chair, speechless, and scrutinized her with a suspicious, questioning gaze, so that she asked: 'What is it?'

'Nothing,' Chéri said. 'I know what I wanted to know.'

She blushed with humiliation, then skilfully defended herself.

'What do you know? That I like your mouth? My poor child, I've kissed uglier. What does that prove? D'you think I'm going to fling myself at your feet and cry, "Take me!" You talk as if you've known only nice young girls! D'you imagine I'm going to lose my head because of a kiss?'

She grew calmer while speaking and wished to prove her self-control.

'Listen, child,' she persisted, as she leaned over him, 'd'you think a handsome mouth means anything to me?'

She smiled down at him, completely sure of herself, but unaware that there remained on her face a sort of very faint quiver, an appealing sadness, and that her smile was like a rainbow after a sudden storm.

'I'm perfectly calm. Even if I were to kiss you again, or even if we ...' She stopped and pouted with scorn. 'No, no, I really can't see you and me doing that.'

'Nor could you see us doing what we did just now,' Chéri said, taking time over his words. 'And yet you don't mind doing it, and not in a hurry, either. So now you're thinking of going further, are you? *I* never suggested such a thing.'

They faced each other like enemies. Léa was afraid to reveal a desire she had not yet had time to develop or to disguise; she resented this child, so suddenly cold and perhaps derisive.

'You're right,' she conceded lightly. 'Let's say no more about it. Shall we say instead that I'm offering to put you out to grass! And the food will be good ... *my* food, in other words.'

'We'll see,' Chéri answered. 'Shall I bring the Renouhard tourer?'

'Of course; you're not going to leave it behind with Charlotte.'

'I'll pay for the petrol, but you'll feed the chauffeur.'

Léa burst out laughing. 'I'll feed the chauffeur! Ha! Ha! There speaks the son of Madame Peloux! Get along with you! You forget nothing. ... I'm not usually inquisitive, but I should love to eavesdrop when you're making up to a woman.'

She sank into a chair and fanned herself. A sphinx-moth and a number of long-legged mosquitoes hovered round the lamps; scents of the countryside drifted in from the garden, now that night had fallen. A sudden waft from an acacia burst in upon them, so distinct, so active, that they both turned round, half expecting to see it advancing towards them.

'It's the rose-acacia,' Léa said.

'Yes,' Chéri said. 'But tonight it has sipped a draught of orange-flower water.'

She stared at him, in vague admiration, astonished that he had hit upon such an idea. He was breathing in the scent in helpless rapture, and she turned away, suddenly fearful lest he might call her; but he did call, and she went to him.

She went to kiss him, on an impulse of resentment and selfishness, and half thinking to chastise him. 'Just you wait, my boy. ... It's all too true that you've a pretty mouth, and, this time, I'm going to take my fill because I want to – and then I'll leave you, I don't care what you may say. Now ...'

Her kiss was such that they reeled apart, drunk, deaf, breathless, trembling as if they had just been fighting. She stood up again in front of him, but he did not move from the depths of his chair, and she taunted him under her breath, 'Well? ... Well?' and waited for an insult. Instead, he held out his arms, opened his vague beautiful hands, tilted his head back as if he had been struck, and let her see beneath each eyelash the glint of a shining tear. He babbled indeterminate words – a whole animal chant of desire, in which she could distinguish her name – 'darling' – 'I want you' – 'I'll never leave you' – a song to which she listened, solicitous, leaning over him, as if unwittingly she had hurt him to the quick.

WHEN Léa recalled their first summer in Normandy, she would sum it up impartially: 'I've had other naughty little boys through my hands, more amusing than Chéri, more likeable, too, and more intelligent. But all the same, never one to touch him.'

'It's funny,' she confided to the old Baron de Berthellemy, towards the end of the summer of 1906, 'but sometimes I think I'm in bed with a Chinee or an African.'

'Have you ever had a Chinaman or a Negro?'

'Never.'

'Well then?'

'I don't know. I can't explain. It's just an impression.'

The impression had grown upon her slowly, also an astonishment she had not always been able to conceal. Her earliest memories of their idyll were abundantly rich, but only in pictures of delicious food, superb fruit, and the pleasure of taking pains over her country larder. She could still see Chéri – paler in the blazing sunlight – dragging along his exhausted body beneath the lime-tree tunnels in Normandy, or asleep on the sun-warmed paving beside a pond.

Léa used to rouse Chéri from sleep to cram him with strawberries and cream, frothy milk, and corn-fed chicken. With wide, vacant eyes, as though dazed, he would sit at dinner watching the mazy motions of the moths round the bowl of roses, and then look at his wrist-watch to see whether the time had come to go to bed: while Léa, disappointed but unresentful, pondered over the unfulfilled promises of the kiss at Neuilly and good-naturedly bided her time.

'I'll keep him cooped up in this fattening-pen till the end of August, if need be. Then, back in Paris again – ouf! – I'll pack him off to his precious studies.'

She went to bed mercifully early, so that Chéri – after nuzzling against her till he had hollowed out a selfishly comfortable position – might get some sleep. Sometimes, when the lamp was out, she would watch a pool of moonlight shimmering over the polished floor, or listen, through the chorus of rustling aspens and shrilling crickets, unceasing by night or day, to the deep, retriever-like sighs that rose from Chéri's breast.

'Why can't I go to sleep? Is there something wrong with me?' she vaguely wondered. 'It's not this boy's head on my shoulder – I've held heavier. The weather's wonderful. I've ordered him a good plate of porridge for tomorrow. Already his ribs stick out less. Then why can't I go to sleep? Yes, of course, I remember. . . . I'm going to send for Patron, the boxer, to give the boy some training. We've plenty of time between us, Patron and I, to spring a surprise on Madame Peloux.'

She fell asleep, lying stretched out on her back between the cool sheets, the dark head of her naughty little boy resting on her left breast. She fell asleep, to be aroused sometimes – but only just – by a waking desire of Chéri's towards the break of day.

Patron actually arrived after they had been two months in their country retreat, with his suitcase, his small pound-and-a-half dumb-bells, his black tights, his six-ounce gloves, and his leather boxing-boots, laced down to the toe. Patron, with his girlish voice, his long eyelashes, and his splendid tanned skin, as brown as the leather of his luggage – he hardly looked naked when he took off his shirt. And Chéri, by turns peevish, listless, or jealous of Patron's smooth strength, started the slow, oft-repeated movements. They were tiresome, but they did him good.

'One . . . sss . . . two . . . sss . . . I can't hear you breathing . . . three . . . sss . . . Don't think I can't see you cheating there with your knee . . . sss . . .'

An awning of lime foliage filtered the August sunlight. The bare bodies of instructor and pupil were dappled with purple reflections from the thick red carpet spread out upon the gravel. Léa watched the lessons with keen attention. Sometimes during the quarter of an hour's boxing, Chéri, drunk with new-found strength, lost all control and, red-faced with anger, attempted a foul blow. Rock-like, Patron stood up to his swings, and from the height of his Olympian glory let fall oracular words – words of wisdom that packed more weight than his proverbial punch.

'Steady on now! That left eye's wandering a bit! If I hadn't

24

stopped myself in time, it would have had a nasty taste of the stitches on my right glove.'

'I slipped,' Chéri said, enraged.

'It's not a question of balance,' Patron went on, 'it's a question of morale. You'll never make a boxer.'

'My mother won't let me, isn't that a pity?'

'Whether your mother lets you or not, you'll never make a boxer, because you've got a rotten temper. Rotten tempers and boxing don't go together. Aren't I right, Madame Léa?'

Léa smiled, and revelled in the warm sun, sitting still and watching the bouts between these two men, both young and both stripped. In her mind she kept comparing them. 'How handsome Patron is – as solid as a house! And the boy's shaping well. You don't find knees like his running about the streets every day of the week, or I'm no judge. His back, too, is ... will be ... marvellous. Where the devil did Mother Peloux drop her line to fish up a child like that? And the set of his head! quite a statue! But what a little beast he is! When he laughs, you'd swear it's a greyhound snarling!' She felt happy and maternal – bathed in quiet virtue. 'I'd willingly change him for anyone else,' she said to herself, with Chéri naked in the afternoon beside her under the lime-tree bower, or with Chéri naked in the morning on her ermine rug, or Chéri naked in the evening on the edge of the warm fountain. 'Yes, handsome as he is, I'd willingly make a change, if it weren't a question of conscience!'

She confessed her indifference to Patron.

'And yet', Patron objected, 'the lad's very nicely made. There's muscles on him now such as you don't see on our French lads; his are more like a coloured boy's – though he couldn't look any whiter, I must say. Nice little muscles they are, and not too showy. He'll never have biceps like melons.'

'I should hope not, Patron! But then, you know, I didn't take him on for his boxing!'

'Of course not,' Patron acquiesced, letting his long lashes droop, 'there's – your feelings to be considered.'

He was always embarrassed by Léa's unveiled allusions to sex, and by her smile – the insistence of the smiling eyes she brought to bear on him whenever she spoke of love.

'Of course,' Patron tried another tack, 'if he's not altogether satisfactory ...'

Léa laughed: 'Altogether! no ... but I find being disinterested is its own reward. Just as you do, Patron.'

'Oh! me ...' He waited in fear and hope for the question that did not fail to follow.

'Always the same, Patron? You still won't give way an inch?'

'I won't give way, Madame Léa, and I've just had a letter from Liane by the midday post. She says she's all alone, that I've no good reasons for refusing, and that her two admirers have left her.'

'Well?'

'Well, I don't believe it! I won't give way, because she won't give way. She's ashamed, she says, of a man who works for his living – specially when it pulls him out of bed so early every day for his training – a man who gives boxing lessons and teaches Swedish gymnastics. We've only got to meet, and the row starts all over again. "Anyone'd think", she shouts at me, "that I'm not in a position to support the man I love!" That shows very nice feelings, I don't say it doesn't, but it doesn't fit in with my ideas. Everyone's funny about something. It's just like you said, Madame Léa, it's all a question of conscience.'

They were talking in low tones under the trees: he prudish and half naked; she dressed in white, the colour flaming in her cheeks. They were enjoying the pleasure of a friendly understanding: they shared the same taste for the simple things of life, good health, and a sort of plebeian decency. And yet Léa would not have been shocked had Patron received handsome presents from a beautiful and expensive woman like Liane. 'Fair exchange is no robbery.' And she did her best to break down Patron's 'funny feelings' by arguments based on homespun justice. These leisurely conversations always revealed their worship of the same twin deities – love and money, and would drift away from money and love to come back to Chéri and his deplorable upbringing, to his exceptional good looks ('harmless, after all,' as Léa would say) and to his character ('virtually nonexistent,' as Léa would say). They had a taste for sharing confidences, and a dislike of new words or ideas, which they satisfied in these long talks. They were often disturbed by the preposterous apparition of

Chéri, whom they thought either asleep or motoring down some baking hot road – Chéri, looming into sight, half naked, but equipped with an account book, a stylo behind his ear.

'Look at our Mister Adding-machine,' Patron said admiringly. 'All got up as a clerk in a bank.'

'What can this mean?' Chéri shouted from afar. 'Three hundred and twenty francs for petrol? Somebody must be swilling the stuff! We've been out four times in the last fortnight – and seventy-seven francs for oil!'

'The motor goes to the market every day,' Léa replied. 'And while we're on the subject, it appears your chauffeur had three helpings of the joint for his dinner. Don't you think that's stretching our agreement a bit far? ... Whenever a bill sticks in your throat, you look just like your mother.'

At a loss for an answer, he stood uncertain for a moment, shifting from one slender foot to the other, poised with winged grace like a young Mercury. This always made Madame Peloux swoon with delight and yelp, 'Me when I was eighteen! Winged feet! winged feet!' He cast about for some insolent retort, his whole face a-quiver, his mouth half open, his forehead jutting forward, in a tense attitude that showed off to advantage the peculiar and diabolic upward twist of his eyebrows.

'Don't bother to think of an answer,' Léa said kindly. 'I know you hate me. Come and kiss me. Handsome devil. Fallen angel. Silly goose. ...'

He came, calmed by the softness of her voice, yet ruffled by her words. Seeing them together, Patron once again let the truth flower on his guileless lips.

'As far as first-rate bodies go, Monsieur Chéri, you have one all right. But whenever I look at it, Monsieur Chéri, I feel that if I was a woman I'd say to myself: "I'll come back again in ten years' time."'

'You hear, Léa? He says in ten years' time,' Chéri said insinuatingly, pushing away the head of his mistress as she leaned towards him. 'What do you think of that?'

But she did not deign to listen. The young body owed to her its renewed vigour, and she began patting it all over, touching it anywhere and everywhere, on the cheek, on the leg, on the behind, with the irreverent pleasure of a nanny.

'What d'you get out of being spiteful?' Patron then asked.

Chéri allowed a savage, inscrutable gaze to sweep over every inch of the waiting Hercules before he answered. 'I find it comforting. You wouldn't understand.'

In fact, Léa herself understood precious little about Chéri after three months' intimacy. If she still talked to Patron, who now came only on Sundays, or to Berthellemy, who arrived without being invited but left again two hours later, about 'sending Chéri back to his blessed studies', it was because the phrase had become a kind of habit, and as though to excuse herself for having kept him there so long. She kept on setting a limit to his stay, and then exceeding it. She was waiting.

'The weather is so lovely. And then his trip to Paris last week tired him. And, besides, it's better for me to get thoroughly sick of him.'

For the first time in her life she waited in vain for what had never before failed her: complete trust on the part of her young lover, a self-surrender to confessions, candours, endless secrets – those hours in the depths of the night when, in almost filial gratitude, a young man unrestrainedly pours out his tears, his private likes and dislikes on the kindly bosom of a mature and trusted friend.

'They've always told me everything in the past,' she thought, obstinately. 'I've always known just what they were worth – what they were thinking and what they wanted. But this boy, this brat ... No, that would really be the limit.'

He was not strong, proud of his nineteen years, gay at meals, and impatient in bed; even so he gave away nothing but his body, and remained as mysterious as an odalisque. Tender? Yes, if an involuntary cry or an impulsive hug is an indication of tenderness. But the moment he spoke, he was 'spiteful' again, careful to divulge nothing of his true self.

How often at dawn had Léa held him in her arms, a lover soothed, relaxed, with half-closed lids! Each morning his eyes and his mouth returned to life more beautiful, as though every waking, every embrace, had fashioned them anew! How often, at such moments, had she indulged her desire to master him, her sensual longing to

28

hear his confession, and pressed her forehead against his, whispering, 'Speak. Say something. Tell me ...'

But no confession came from those curved lips, scarcely anything indeed but sulky or frenzied phrases woven round 'Nounoune' – the name he had given her when a child and the one he now used in the throes of his pleasure, almost like a cry for help.

'Yes, I assure you, he might be a Chinee, or an African,' she declared to Anthime de Berthellemy, and added, 'I can't tell you why.' The impression was strong but confused, and she felt lazily incompetent to find words for the feeling that she and Chéri did not speak the same language.

It was the end of September when they returned to Paris. Chéri went straight to Neuilly, the very first evening, to 'spring a surprise' on Madame Peloux. He brandished chairs, cracked nuts with his fist, leaped on to the billiard-table, and played cowboy in the garden at the heels of the terrified watch-dogs.

'Ouf!' Léa sighed, as she entered her house in the Avenue Bugeaud, alone. 'How wonderful! – a bed to myself!'

But at ten o'clock the following night she was sipping coffee and trying not to find the evening too long or the dining-room too large, when a nervous cry was forced from her lips. Chéri had suddenly appeared, framed in the doorway – Chéri, wafted on silent, winged feet.

He was not speaking or showing any sign of affection, but just running towards her.

'Are you mad?'

Shrugging his shoulders, disdaining all explanations, just running towards her. Never asking 'Do you love me?', 'Have you already forgotten me?' Running towards her.

A moment later they were lying in the middle of Léa's great brass-encumbered bed. Chéri pretended to be worn out and sleepy. This made it easier to grit his teeth and keep his eyes tight shut, suffering as he was from a furious attack of taciturnity. Yet, through his silence, she was listening as she lay beside him, listening with delight to the distant delicate vibration, to the imprisoned tumult thrumming within a body that sought to conceal its agony, its gratitude, and love.

'Why didn't your mother tell me this herself at dinner last night?'

'She thought it better it should come from me.'

'No!'

'That's what she said.'

'And you?'

'What about me?'

'Do you think it better?'

Chéri raised uncertain eyes to Léa's. 'Yes.' He appeared to think it over a moment and repeated: 'Yes, far better, in fact.'

In order not to embarrass him, Léa looked away towards the window.

The August morning was dark with warm rain, which fell vertically on the already rusted foliage of the three plane trees in the garden court.

'It might be autumn,' she said, and sighed.

'What's the matter?' Chéri asked.

She looked at him in astonishment. 'Nothing, I don't like the rain, that's all.'

'Oh! All right, I thought ...'

'What?'

'I thought something was wrong.'

She could not help giving a frank laugh. 'Wrong with me, because you're getting married? No, listen ... you're ... you're so funny.'

She seldom laughed outright, and her merriment vexed Chéri. He shrugged his shoulders and made the usual grimace while lighting a cigarette, jutting out his chin too far and protruding his lower lip.

'You oughtn't to smoke before luncheon,' Léa said.

He made some impertinent retort she did not hear. She was listening to the sound of her own voice and its daily lectures, echoing away down the past five years. 'It's like the endless repetition in opposite looking-glasses,' she thought. Then, with a slight effort, she returned to reality and cheerfulness.

'It's lucky for me that there'll soon be someone else to stop you smoking on an empty stomach.'

'Oh! *she* won't be allowed to have a say in anything,' Chéri declared. 'She's going to be my wife, isn't she? Let her kiss the sacred ground I tread on, and thank her lucky stars for the privilege. And that will be that.'

He exaggerated the thrust of his chin, clenched his teeth on his cigarette-holder, parted his lips, and, as he stood there in his white silk pyjamas, succeeded only in looking like an Asiatic prince grown pale in the impenetrable obscurity of palaces.

Léa drew the folds of her pink dressing-gown closer about her – the pink she called 'indispensable'. She was lazily turning over ideas which she found tiresome, ideas that she decided to hurl, one by one, as missiles against Chéri's assumed composure.

'Well, why are you marrying the child?'

He put both elbows on the table and, unconsciously, assumed the composed features of his mother. 'Well, you see, my dear girl ...'

'Call me Madame or Léa. I'm neither your housemaid nor a pal of your own age.'

She sat straight up in her armchair and clipped her words without raising her voice. He wanted to answer back. He looked defiantly at the beautiful face, a little pale under its powder, and at the frank blue light of her searching eyes. But he softened, and conceded, in a tone most unusual for him, 'Nounoune, you asked me to explain. ... It had to come to this in the end. And besides, there are big interests at stake.'

'Whose?'

'Mine,' he said without a smile. 'The girl has a considerable fortune of her own.'

'From her father?'

He rocked himself to and fro, his feet in the air. 'Oh, how do I know? What a question! I suppose so. You'd hardly expect the fair Marie-Laure to draw fifteen hundred thousand out of her own bank account, would you? Fifteen hundred thousand, and some decent family jewels into the bargain.'

'And how much have you?'

'Oh, I've more than that of my own,' he said with pride.

'Then you don't need any more money?'

He shook his smooth head and it caught the light like blue watered silk. 'Need ... need ...? You know perfectly well we don't look at money in the same way. It's something on which we never see eye to eye.'

'I'll do you the justice to say that you've spared me any reference to it during the last five years.' She leaned towards him and put her hand on his knee. 'Tell me, child, how much have you put by from your income in these five years?'

He cavorted like a clown, laughed, and rolled at Léa's feet, but she pushed him aside with her toe.

'No, tell me the truth ... fifty thousand a year, or sixty? Tell me, sixty? Seventy?'

He sat down on the carpet facing away from Léa, and laid his head back on her lap. 'Aren't I worth it, then?'

He stretched out to his full length, turned his head to look up at her, and opened wide his eyes. They looked black, but their true shade, Léa knew, was a dark almost reddish brown. As though to indicate her choice of what was rarest among so much beauty, she put her forefinger on his eyebrows, his eyelids, and the corners of his mouth. At moments this lover, whom she slightly despised, inspired her with a kind of respect by his outward form. 'To be as handsome as that amounts to nobility,' she said to herself.

'Tell me, child, how does this young person feel about you?'

'She loves me. She admires me. She never says a word.'

'And you – how do you behave with her?'

'I don't,' he answered simply.

'Delightful love duets,' Léa said dreamily.

He sat up, crossing his legs tailor fashion.

'You seem to me to be thinking a lot about her,' he said severely. 'Don't you think of yourself at all, in this upheaval?'

She gazed at Chéri with an astonishment that made her look years younger – eyebrows raised and lips half open.

'Yes, you, Léa. You, the victimized heroine. You, the one sympathetic character in all this, since you're being dropped.'

He had become rather pale, and his tough handling of Léa seemed to be hurting him.

32

Léa smiled. 'But, my darling, I've not the slightest intention of changing my life. Now and then, during the next week, I'll come across a pair of socks, a tie, a handkerchief on my shelves ... and when I say a week .. you know in what excellent order my shelves are kept! Oh, yes, and I'll have the bathroom redone. I've got an idea of putting in encrusted glass. ...'

She fell silent and assumed an almost greedy look as she traced a vague outline with her finger. Chéri continued to look vindictive.

'You aren't pleased! What do you want, then? Do you expect me to go to Normandy to hide my grief? To pine away? To stop dyeing my hair? To have Madame Peloux rushing to my bedside?' And she imitated Madame Peloux, flapping her arms and trumpeting: ' "The shadow of her former self, the shadow of her former self! The poor unfortunate creature has aged a hundred years, a hundred years!" Is that what you want?'

He had been listening with a smile that died on his lips, and a trembling of the nostrils that might be due to emotion. 'Yes!' he cried.

Léa rested her smooth, bare, heavy arms on Chéri's shoulders.

'My poor boy! But at that rate, I ought to have died four or five times already! To lose a little lover. ... To exchange one naughty little boy. ...' She added in lower, lighter tones: 'I've grown used to it!'

'We all know that,' he said harshly. 'I don't give a damn – d'you hear me? – I don't give a single damn that I wasn't your first lover. What I should have liked, or rather what would have been ... fitting ... decent ... is to be your last.' With a twist of his shoulders, he shrugged off her superb arms. 'After all, what I am saying to you now is for your own good.'

'I understand perfectly. You think only of me. I think only of your fiancée. That's all very nice, all very natural. It's clear that we both have hearts of gold.'

She rose, waiting for some outrageous rejoinder. But he said nothing, and it hurt her to see for the first time a look of discouragement on his face.

She bent over and put her hands under his armpits.

'Now then, come along, get your clothes on. I've only to put on

33

my dress, I'm ready underneath, and what in the world is there to do on a day like this except to go to Schwabe and choose a pearl for you? You see, I must give you a wedding present.'

He jumped up, his face aglow: 'Top-hole! A pearl for my shirt-front! A pale pink pearl. I know the very one!'

'Not on your life! A white one, something masculine for pity's sake! Don't tell me, I know which one just as well as you. It'll ruin me, as usual. However, think of the money I'm going to save when you're out of the way!'

Chéri adopted a more reticent attitude. 'Oh, that ... that depends on my successor.'

Léa turned back at the door of her boudoir and gave him her gayest smile, showing her strong teeth and the fresh blue of her eyes skilfully darkened by bistre.

'Your successor? A couple of francs and a packet of cigarettes! And a glass of cassis on Sunday – that's all the job will be worth! And I'll settle money on your children.'

THEY both became extremely gay for the next few weeks. Chéri's official duties as a fiancé separated them for a few hours each day, sometimes for a night or two. 'We mustn't let them lose confidence,' Chéri declared. Léa, kept by Madame Peloux at a safe distance from Neuilly, satisfied her curiosity by plying Chéri with a hundred questions. Whenever he came back to Léa's house, he was full of his own importance and heavy with secrets which he at once divulged. He was like a schoolboy playing truant.

'Oh, my sainted aunt!' he shouted one day, cramming his hat down on Léa's portrait-bust. 'The goings-on at the Peloux Palace Hôtel ever since yesterday!'

She began by scolding him, laughing already in anticipation.

'Take your hat off that, in the first place. And in the second, don't invoke your wretched aunt in my house. Well, what's been happening now?'

'A riot, Nounoune! A riot's broken out among the ladies. Marie-Laure and Ma'me Peloux are scratching each other's eyes out over the marriage settlement!'

'No!'

'Yes! It was a superb sight. (Look out for the olives. ... I'm going to impersonate Ma'me Peloux as a windmill. ...) "Separate bank accounts! Separate bank accounts! Why not a trustee? It's a personal insult, a personal insult. You forget that my son has his own fortune! ... May I inform you, Madame..."'

'She called her Madame?'

'She most certainly did. "Let me tell you, Madame, that my son has never had a ha'porth of debts since he came of age and the list of his investments bought since 1910 is worth ..." is worth this, that, and the other, including the skin off my nose, plus the fat off my bottom. In short, Catherine de Medici in person! But even more artful, of course!'

Léa's blue eyes glistened with tears of merriment. 'Oh, Chéri! you've never been funnier in your life! What about the other? The fair Marie-Laure?'

'Her? Oh! terrible, Nounoune. That woman must have at least a dozen corpses in her wake. Dolled up in jade green, red hair, painted to look eighteen, and the inevitable smile. The trumpetings of my revered Mamma failed to make her bat an eyelid. She held her fire till the assault was over, then she came out with: "It might perhaps be wiser, dear Madame, not to talk too loudly about all the money your son put by in 1910 and the years following. ..." '

'Bang! Straight between the eyes! ... Between yours. Where were you while all this was going on?'

'Me? In the large armchair.'

'You were actually in the room?' She stopped laughing, and eating. 'You were there? What did you do?'

'Cracked a joke, of course. Ma'me Peloux had just seized hold of a valuable piece of bric-à-brac, to avenge my honour, when I stopped her without even getting up. "My adored mother, calm yourself. Follow my example, follow that of my charming mother-in-law, who's being as sweet as honey ... as sweet as sugar." And that's how I managed to arrange that the settlement should apply only to property acquired after marriage.'

'I simply don't understand.'

'The famous sugar plantations that the poor little Prince Ceste left to Marie-Laure by his will. ...'

'Yes?'

'Forged will! Fury of the Ceste family! Lawsuit pending! Now d'you get it?'

He crowed.

'I get it. But how did you get hold of the story?'

'Ah! I'll tell you! Old Lili has just pounced with her full weight upon the younger of the Ceste boys, who's only seventeen and religious. ...'

'Old Lili? What a nightmare!'

'And he babbles family secrets in her ear between every kiss. ...'

'Chéri! I feel sick!'

'And old Lili tipped me off at Mamma's At Home last Sunday. She simply adores me! Besides, she respects me because I've never wanted to go to bed with her. ...'

'I should hope not!' Léa sighed. 'Yet all the same ...' She broke off to reflect, and it seemed to Chéri her enthusiasm was flagging.

'Well, you must say it was pretty smart of me, eh?'

He leaned across the table; and the sunshine, playing over the silver and the white table-cloth, lit him up like a row of footlights.

'Yes ...' 'All the same,' she was thinking, 'that poisonous Marie-Laure simply treated him like a ponce. ...'

'Is there any cream cheese, Nounoune?'

'Yes ...' '... and he showed no more surprise than if she had thrown him a flower. ...'

'Nounoune, will you let me have that address? the address of the place where you get your cream cheese – for the new cook I've engaged for October?'

'Are you mad? It's home-made. I *have* a cook, you know. Think of the *sauce aux moules* and *vol-au-vent*!' '... it's true I've practically kept the boy for the last five years. ... But all the same he has an income of three hundred thousand francs a year. That's the point. Can you be a ponce with three hundred thousand a year? But why ever not? It doesn't depend on the amount, but on the man. ... There are some men I could have given half a million to, and that wouldn't make them a ponce. But how about Chéri? After all, I have never actually given him any money. All the same ...'

'All the same,' she broke into speech. 'She treated you like a gigolo!'

'Who did?'

'Marie-Laure!'

He brightened at once, like a child.

'Didn't she? Didn't she just, Nounoune? That's what she meant, wasn't it?'

'So it seems to me.'

Chéri raised his glass of Château-Chalon, almost the colour of brandy. 'So here's to Marie-Laure! What a compliment, eh? And if anyone can still say it of me when I'm your age, I shan't ask anything better!'

'If that's enough to make you happy ...'

She listened to him absent-mindedly till the end of luncheon. Accustomed to her half-silences and her worldly wisdom, he asked for nothing better than the usual maternal homilies – 'Take the brownest crusts. Don't eat so much new bread. ... You've never learnt how to choose a fruit. ...' All the time, secretly disgruntled, she was reproaching herself, 'I must make up my mind what I want! What would I really have liked him to do? Get up on his hind legs and hiss "Madame, you have insulted me! Madame, I am not what you take me for!" I'm responsible, when all's said and done. I've spoon-fed him, I've stuffed him with good things. ... Who in the world would have thought that one day he'd want to play the paterfamilias? It never occurred to me! Even supposing it had – as Patron would say, "Nature will out." Even supposing Patron had accepted Liane's proposals, his nature would have come out all right if anyone had hinted at the fact in his hearing. But Chéri ... has Chéri's nature. He's just Chéri. He's –'

'What were you saying, child?' she interrupted her thoughts to ask. 'I wasn't listening.'

'I was saying that never again – never, do you hear me – will anything make me laugh so much as my scene with Marie-Laure!'

– 'There you are,' Léa concluded her thoughts, 'it ... it merely made him laugh.'

Slowly she rose to her feet, as though tired. Chéri put an arm round her waist, but she pushed it away.

'What day is your wedding to be, now I come to think of it?'

'Monday week.'

His candour and detachment terrified her. 'That's fantastic!'

'Why fantastic, Nounoune?'

'You don't look as if you were giving it a thought!'

'I'm not,' he said calmly. 'Everything's been arranged. Ceremony at two o'clock, saving us all the fuss and rush of a wedding breakfast. Instead, a tea-party at Ma'me Peloux's. After that, sleepers, Italy, the Lakes. ...'

'Are the Lakes back in fashion?'

'They are. There'll be villas, hotels, motor drives, restaurants, like Monte Carlo, eh?'

'But the girl! There's always the girl. ...'

'Of course there's the girl. She's not much, but she's there!'

'And I'm no longer there.'

Chéri had not expected her to say this and showed it. His face became disfigured, and he suddenly turned white about the mouth. He controlled his breath to avoid an audible gasp, and became himself again.

'Nounoune, you'll always be there.'

'Monsieur overwhelms me.'

'There'll always be you, Nounoune ...' and he laughed awkwardly, 'whenever I need you to do something for me.'

She did not answer. She bent to pick up a tortoiseshell comb that had fallen to the floor and pushed it back in her hair, humming to herself. She went on humming a little snatch of a song in front of a looking-glass, pleased with herself, proud of having kept her self-control so easily, covered up so successfully the only emotional moment of their separation, proud of having held back words that must never be said: 'Speak ... beg for what you want, demand it, put your arms round my neck. ... You have suddenly made me happy. ...'

MADAME PELOUX must have been talking a great deal and for a long time before Léa appeared. The high colour on her cheeks emphasized the sparkle of her large eyes, which expressed only an indiscreet and inscrutable watchfulness. This Sunday she was wearing a black afternoon dress with a very narrow skirt, and nobody could fail to have observed that her feet were tiny and her stays too tight. She stopped talking, took a little sip from the petal-thin brandy glass warming in her hand, and nodded at Léa in lazy contentment.

'Isn't it a lovely day? Such weather, such weather! Would anyone believe we're in the middle of October?'

'Oh, no, never. ... Most certainly not!' two obsequious voices answered in chorus.

Beside the curving garden path a stream of red salvias wound between the banks of grey-mauve Michaelmas daisies. Golden butterflies flitted as if it were summer and the scent of chrysanthemums, strengthened by the hot sun, was wafted into the garden-room. A yellowing birch-tree trembled in the wind above beds of tea-roses, where the last of the bees still were busy.

'But what's this weather,' yelled Madame Peloux, suddenly waxing lyrical, 'but what's this weather, when compared to what *they* must be having in Italy?'

'Yes, indeed! ... Just what I was thinking!' the attendant voices echoed.

Léa turned with a frown in their direction. 'If only they would hold their tongues,' she thought.

The Baroness de la Berche and Madame Aldonza were sitting at a card-table, playing piquet. Madame Aldonza, an aged ballerina, with legs eternally swathed in bandages, was distorted with rheumatism, and wore her shiny black wig a little askew. Opposite her, a head or more taller, the Baroness squared her rigid shoulders like a country priest's. Her face was large and had grown alarmingly masculine with age. She was a bristling bush of hair – hair in her ears, tufts in her nostrils and on her lip, and rough hairs between her fingers.

'Baroness, don't forget I made ninety,' Madame Aldonza bleated like a goat.

'Score it, score it, my good friend! All I want is to see everyone happy.'

An endless flow of honied words masked her savage cruelty. Léa looked at her closely as if for the first time, felt disgusted, and turned back to Madame Peloux. 'Charlotte, at least, *looks* human,' she thought.

'What's the matter with you, my Léa? You don't seem your usual self?' Madame Peloux inquired tenderly.

Léa drew up her handsome figure and answered: 'Of course I am, Lolotte dear ... it's so comfortable here in your house, I was merely relaxing, thinking all the while "Careful now ... she's just as cruel as the other"', and she at once assumed an expression of flattering contentment, of dreamy repletion, and accentuated it by sighing, 'I lunched too well ... I really must get thinner. I shall start a strict diet from tomorrow.'

Madame Peloux flapped her hands and simpered.

'Isn't a broken heart enough to do that?'

'Oh, oh, oh! Ha-ha! Ho-ho!' guffawed Madame Aldonza and the Baroness de la Berche. 'Ha-ha-ha!'

Léa rose to her full height in her autumn dress of sombre green, handsome under her satin hat trimmed with sealskin, youthful among these old ruins over whom she cast a gentle eye. 'Oh, la-la, my dears! Give me a dozen such heart-breaks, if that would help me to lose a couple of pounds!'

'Léa, you're astounding,' the old baroness shot at her in a puff of smoke. 'Madame Léa, think of me, please, when you throw away that hat,' old Madame Aldonza begged. 'Madame Charlotte, you remember your blue one? It lasted me two years. Baroness, when you've quite finished ogling Madame Léa, perhaps you'll be kind enough to deal the cards to me.'

'Very well, my sweet, and may they bring you luck!'

Léa stopped for a moment by the door, then stepped out into the garden. She picked a tea-rose, which shed its petals. She listened to the breeze in the birch, to the trams in the Avenue, to the whistle of the local train. The bench she sat on was warm, and she closed her eyes, letting her shoulders enjoy the warmth of the sun. When she opened her eyes again, she hurriedly turned her head in the direction of the house, feeling positive that she was going to see Chéri standing in the entrance with his shoulder against the doorway.

'What can be the matter with me?' she wondered. Piercing screams of laughter and a little chorus of greeting from indoors brought her, trembling slightly, to her feet. 'Can I be suffering from nerves!'

'Ah, here they are, here they are!' Madame Peloux trumpeted, and the deep bass of the Baroness chimed in 'Here come the happy pair!'

Léa shivered, ran as far as the door, and stopped short: there, in front of her, were old Lili and her adolescent lover, Prince Ceste, just arriving.

Perhaps seventy years of age, with the corpulence of a eunuch held in by stays, old Lili was usually referred to as 'passing all bounds', without these 'bounds' being defined. Her round pink painted face was enlivened by a ceaseless girlish gaiety, and her large eyes and small mouth, thin-lipped and shrunken, flirted shamelessly. Old Lili followed the fashion to an outrageous degree. A striking blue-and-white striped skirt held in the lower part of her body, and a little blue jersey gaped over her skinny bosom crinkled like the wattles of a turkey-cock; a silver fox failed to conceal the neck, which was the shape of a flower-pot and the size of a belly. It had engulfed the chin.

'It's terrifying,' Léa thought. She was unable to tear her eyes away from details that were particularly sinister – a white sailor hat, for instance, girlishly perched on the back of a short-cut, strawberry-roan wig; or, again, a pearl necklace visible one moment and the next interred in a deep ravine which once had been termed a *collier de Vénus*.

'Léa, Léa, my little chickabiddy!' old Lili exclaimed as she did her best to hasten towards Léa. She walked with difficulty on round swollen feet, tightly swaddled in high-heeled laced boots with paste buckles on the ankle-straps, and was the first to congratulate herself on this performance: 'I waddle like a duckling! it is a special little way I have. Guido, my passion, you remember Madame de Lonval? Don't remember her too well or I'll tear your eyes out. ...'

A slim youth with Italian features, enormous empty eyes, and a weak receding chin kissed Léa's hand hastily and retired into the shadows without a word. Lili caught him in flight, pulled his head down to her scaly chest, calling the onlookers to witness: 'Do you know what this is, Madame, do you know what this is? This, ladies, is the love of my life!'

'Restrain yourself, Lili!' Madame de la Berche advised in her masculine voice.

'But why? But why?' from Charlotte Peloux.

'For the sake of decency,' said the Baroness.

'Baroness, that's not nice of you! I think they're so sweet. Ah!' she sighed, 'they remind me of my own children.'

'I was thinking of them,' Lili said, with a delighted smile. 'It's our honeymoon too, Guido's and mine. Indeed, we've just come to ask about the other young couple! We want to hear all about them.'

Madame Peloux became stern. 'Lili, you don't expect me to go into details, do you?'

'Oh, yes, yes, I do,' Lili cried, clapping her hands. She tried to skip, but succeeded only in raising her shoulders and hips a little. 'That's always been my besetting sin, and always will be! I adore spicy talk! I'll never be cured of it. That little wretch there knows how I adore it.'

The silent youth, called to bear witness, did not open his mouth. The black pupils of his eyes moved up and down against the whites, like frantic insects. Léa watched him, rooted to the spot.

'Madame Charlotte told us all about the wedding ceremony,' bleated Madame Aldonza. 'The young Madame Peloux was a dream in her wreath of orange blossom!'

'A madonna! A madonna!' Madame Peloux corrected at the top of her voice, with a burst of religious fervour. 'Never, never, has anyone looked so divine. My son was in heaven! In heaven, I tell you! ... What a pair they made, what a pair!'

'You hear that, my passion? Orange blossom!' Lili murmured. 'And tell me, Charlotte, what about our mother-in-law, Marie-Laure?'

Madame Peloux's pitiless eyes sparkled: 'Oh, her! Out of place, absolutely out of place. In tight-fitting black, like an eel wriggling out of the water – you could see everything, breasts, stomach – everything!'

'By Jove!' muttered the Baroness de la Berche with military gusto.

'And that look of contempt she has for everybody, that look of having a dose of cyanide up her sleeve and half a pint of chloroform inside her handbag! As I said, out of place – that exactly describes her. She behaved as if she could only spare us five minutes of her precious time – she'd hardly brushed the kiss off her lips, before she said, "Au revoir, Edmée, au revoir, Fred," and off she flew.'

Old Lili was breathing hard, sitting on the edge of her chair, her little grandmotherly mouth, with its puckered corners, hanging half open. 'And who gave the usual advice?' she threw out.

'What advice?'

'The little talk – oh, my passion, hold my hand while I say it! – instruction for the young bride. Who gave her that?'

Charlotte Peloux took offence and stared at her. 'Things may well have been done in that way when you were young, but the practice has fallen into disuse.'

The sprightly old girl plumped her fists on her thighs: 'Disuse? Disuse or not, how would you know anything about it, my poor Charlotte? There's so little marrying in your family!'

'Ha-ha-ha!' the two toadies imprudently guffawed.

But a single glance from Madame Peloux made them tremble. 'Peace, peace, my little angels! You're each enjoying your paradise on earth, so what more do you want?' The Baroness stretched out a strong arm, like a policeman keeping order, between the purple faces of Lili and Madame Peloux. But Charlotte scented battle like a war-horse. 'If you're looking for trouble, Lili, you don't have to look further than me! Because of your age, I must treat you with respect, and if it weren't for that ...'

Lili shook with laughter from chin to thigh. 'If it weren't for that, you'd get married yourself just to give me the lie? I know – it's not so hard to get married! Why, I'd marry Guido like a shot, if only he were of age!'

'Not possible!' gasped Charlotte, so taken aback that she forgot her anger.

'But, of course ... Princess Ceste, my dear! *la piccola principessa! Piccola principessa*, that's what my little Prince always calls me!'

She nipped hold of her skirt, and, in turning, displayed as gold curb-chain where her ankle ought to have been. 'Only', she continued mysteriously, 'his father ...'

By now out of breath, she made a sign to that silent young man, who took up the tale in a low rapid voice as if he were reciting his piece: 'My father, the Duke of Parese, threatens to put me in a convent if I marry Lili.'

'In a convent!' Charlotte Peloux squealed. 'A man in a convent!'

'A man in a convent!' neighed Madame de la Berche in her deep bass. 'Egad! if that isn't exciting!'

'They're barbarians,' Aldonza lamented, joining her misshapen hands together.

Léa rose so abruptly that she upset a glass.

'It's uncoloured glass,' Madame Peloux observed with satisfaction. 'You'll bring good luck to my young couple. Where are you running off to? Is your house on fire?'

Léa managed to squeeze out a sly little laugh: 'On fire? In a sense, perhaps. Ssh! no questions! It's a secret.'

'What? Already? It's not possible!' Charlotte Peloux cheeped enviously. 'I was just saying to myself that you looked as if ...'

'Yes, yes! You must tell us! Tell us everything,' yapped the three old women.

Lili's quilted fists, old Aldonza's deformed stumps, Charlotte Peloux's hard fingers had seized upon her wrist, her sleeve, her gold-mesh bag. She snatched her arms away from all these claws and succeeded in laughing again, teasingly: 'No, it's far too early in the day, it would spoil everything! It's my secret.' And she rushed away to the hall.

But the door opened in front of her and a desiccated old fellow, a sort of playful mummy, took her into his arms: 'Léa, lovely creature, a kiss for your little Berthellemy, or he won't let you pass!'

She gave a cry of fright and impatience, struck off the gloved bones retarding her progress, and fled.

45

Neither in the avenues of Neuilly, nor on the roads through the Bois, turning to blue in the fast-falling twilight, did she allow herself a moment's reflection. She shivered slightly and pulled up the windows of the motor-car. She felt restored by the sight of her clean house, the comfort of her pink bedroom and boudoir, overcrowded with furniture and flowers.

'Quick, Rose, light the fire in my room!'

'But, Madame, the pipes are already at their winter temperature. Madame should not have gone out with only a fur round her neck. The evenings are treacherous.'

'A hot-water bottle in my bed at once, and for dinner a cup of thick chocolate beaten up with the yolk of an egg, some toast, and a bunch of grapes. ... Hurry, dear, I'm freezing. I caught cold in that junk-shop at Neuilly. ...'

Once under the sheets, she clenched her teeth to stop them chattering. The warmth of the bed eased her stiffened muscles, but still she did not altogether relax, and she went through the chauffeur's expense book till the chocolate arrived. This she drank at once, frothy and scalding. She chose her *chasselas* grapes one by one, the long greenish-amber bunch dangling by its stem against the light.

Then she turned out the bedside lamp, settled herself in her favourite position, flat on her back, and gave way.

'What can be the matter with me?'

She succumbed again to anxiety and started to shiver. She was obsessed by the vision of an empty doorway, with clumps of red salvia on either side. 'I can't be well,' she thought, 'one doesn't get into a state like this over a door!' Again she saw the three old women, Lili's neck, and the beige rug that Madame Aldonza had trailed about with her for the past twenty years. 'Which of them am I going to look like in ten years' time?'

Though she did not feel alarmed at this prospect, her anxiety increased still further. She let her mind wander from one incident of her past life to another, from this scene to that, trying to rid her thoughts of the empty doorway framed by red salvia. She was growing restless in her bed and trembled slightly. Suddenly she jumped as though shot, racked by a pain so deep that at first she thought it must be physical, a pain that twisted her lips and dragged from them, in a raucous sob, a single name: 'Chéri!'

Tears followed, beyond all control at first. As soon as she had regained her self-control, she sat up, wiped her face, and turned on the lamp again. 'Ah! That's what it is! Now I understand!'

She took a thermometer from the drawer of her bedside table and put it under her arm. 'My temperature's normal, so it's nothing physical. I see. I'm just unhappy. Something must be done about it.'

She drank some water, got out of bed, bathed her inflamed eyes, put on a little powder, poked the fire, and went back to bed. She was on her guard, full of mistrust for an enemy she had never known: grief. She had just said goodbye to thirty years of easy living: years spent pleasantly, intent often on love, sometimes on money. This had left her, at almost fifty, still young and defenceless.

She made fun of herself, ceased to feel her grief, and smiled. 'I think I was out of my mind just now. There's nothing wrong with me any longer.'

But a movement of her left arm, which bent automatically to hold and shelter a sleeping head, brought back all her agony, and she sat up with a jump. 'Well, this *is* going to be fun!' she said out loud and sternly.

She looked at the clock and saw that it was barely eleven. Overhead passed the slippered tread of the elderly Rose, on her way up the stairs to the attic floor. Then there was silence. Léa resisted the impulse to call out for help to this deferential old body. 'Don't give the servants anything to gossip about. We mustn't have that.'

She left her bed again, wrapped herself up warm in a quilted silk dressing-gown and toasted her feet. Then she half opened her window and listened for she knew not what. A moist and milder wind had brought clouds in its wake, and the lingering leaves in the neighbouring Bois sighed with every gust. Léa shut the window again, picked up a newspaper, and looked at the date – 'October the twenty-sixth. Exactly a month since Chéri was married?' She never said 'Since Edmée was married'.

Following Chéri's example, she did not yet count his young wraith of a wife as really alive. Chestnut-brown eyes, ashy hair which

47

was very lovely with the vestige of a crimp in it – all the rest melted away in her memory like the contours of a face seen in a dream.

'At this very moment, of course, they'll be in each other's arms in Italy. And ... and I don't mind that in the least.'

She was not boasting. The picture of the young couple she had called up, the familiar attitude it evoked – even Chéri's face, as he lay exhausted for a minute, with the white line of light between his tired eyelids – aroused in her neither curiosity nor jealousy. On the other hand, an animal convulsion again racked her body, bending her double, as her eyes fell on a nick in the pearl-grey wainscot – the mark of some brutality of Chéri's. 'The lovely hand which here has left its trace, has turned away from me for ever,' she said. 'How grandly I'm talking! Soon grief will be turning me into a poet!'

She walked about, she sat down, she went to bed again, and waited for daylight. At eight o'clock Rose found her writing at her desk, and this upset the old lady's-maid.

'Is Madame not well?'

'So-so, Rose. Age, you know. ... Doctor Vidal thinks I ought to have a change of air. Will you come with me? It promises to be a cold winter here in Paris. We'll go south to the sun, and eat meals cooked in oil.'

'Whereabouts will that be?'

'You want to know too much. Simply have my trunks brought down, and give my fur rugs a good beating.'

'Madame will be taking the motor-car?'

'I think so. I'm sure of it, in fact. I'll need all my creature comforts now, Rose. Just think of it, this time I'm going all on my own. It's going to be a pleasure trip.'

During the next five days Léa rushed all over Paris; wrote, telegraphed, and received telegrams and answers from the south. And she said goodbye to Paris, leaving behind a short letter addressed to Madame Peloux which she started no less than three times:

My dear Charlotte,

You'll forgive me if I go away without saying goodbye to you, and keep my little secret to myself. I'm making a perfect fool of myself ... and why not? It's a short life, let's make it a gay one.

I send you an affectionate kiss. Remember me to the child when he comes back.

Your incorrigible

Léa.

P.S. — Don't trouble to come and interview my butler or concierge, no member of my household knows anything at all about it.

'Do you know, my adored treasure, I don't think you're looking very well.'

'It's the night in the train,' Chéri answered shortly.

Madame Peloux did not dare to say just what she thought. She found her son changed. 'He's ... yes, he's sinister!' she decided; and she ended by exclaiming enthusiastically, 'It's Italy!'

'If you like,' Chéri conceded.

Mother and son had just finished breakfasting together, and Chéri had condescended to praise with an oath his cup of 'housemaid's coffee', made with creamy milk, well sugared, slowly reheated, with buttered toast crumbled into it and browned till it formed a succulent crust.

He felt cold in his white woollen pyjamas and was clasping his knees to his chest. Charlotte Peloux, anxious to look pretty for her son, had put on a brand-new marigold négligée, and a boudoir-cap fitting tight across the forehead. This made her face stand out, bare and macabre.

Finding her son's eye fixed upon her, she simpered: 'You see, I've adopted the grandmother style. Very soon, I'll powder my hair. Do you like this cap? Rather eighteenth century, don't you think? Dubarry or Pompadour? How do I look in it?'

'Like an old convict,' Chéri said witheringly. 'Next time you must run up a warning signal.'

She groaned, then shrieked with laughter: 'Ha-ha-ha. You've a sharp tongue in your head and no mistake!'

But he did not laugh. He was staring out at the lawn powdered with snow after last night's fall. His nervous state was visible only in the spasmodic twitching of his jaw muscles. Madame Peloux was intimidated. She, too, was silent. The faint tinkle of a bell sounded.

'That's Edmée, ringing for her breakfast,' said Madame Peloux.

Chéri did not answer. 'What's wrong with the heating? It's freezing in here!' he said a moment later.

'It's Italy!' Madame Peloux repeated lyrically. 'You come back here, your eyes and your heart full of the warm sun of the south, and find you've landed at the Pole – at the North Pole. There hasn't been a flower on the dahlias for the last week. But don't worry, my precious! Your love-nest will soon be finished. If the architect hadn't gone down with paratyphoid, it would be ready for you now. I warned him. If I told him once, I told him twenty times: "Monsieur Savaron ..."'

Chéri, who was standing by the window, turned round sharply. 'What was the date on that letter?'

Madame Peloux opened her large childlike eyes: 'What letter?'

'The letter from Léa you showed me.'

'She put no date on it, my love; but I got it the night before my last Sunday At Home in October.'

'I see. And you don't know who it is?'

'Who what is, my paragon?'

'Whoever it was she went away with, of course.'

Malice clothed Madame Peloux's stark features. 'No. Would you believe it, nobody has an idea! Old Lili is in Sicily, and none of my set has a clue! A mystery, an enthralling mystery! However, you know me, I've managed to pick up a few scraps here and there ...'

Chéri's dark eyes expanded: 'What's the tattle?'

'It seems it's a young man ...' Madame Peloux whispered. 'A young man not ... not particularly desirable, if you know what I mean ... very well made, of course!' She was lying, careful to insinuate the worst.

Chéri shrugged his shoulders.

'Well made, did you say? Don't make me laugh! My poor Léa! I can see him from here – a hefty little fellow from Patron's training-quarters – black hairs on his wrists and clammy hands. ... Well, I'm going back to bed now; you make me tired.'

Trailing his bedroom slippers, he went back to his room, dawdling in the long corridors and on the spacious landings of the house he seemed to be discovering for the first time. He ran into a pot-bellied wardrobe, and was amazed. 'Damned if I knew that thing was there. ... Oh, yes, I vaguely remember. ... And who the devil's this chap?' He was addressing an enlarged photograph, in a deep black frame, hanging funereally near a piece of coloured pottery, equally unfamiliar to Chéri.

Madame Peloux had been installed in this house for the last twenty-five years, and had kept every unfortunate result of her bad taste and acquisitiveness. 'Your house looks like the nest of a magpie that's gone batty,' was old Lili's reproachful comment. She herself had a hearty appetite for modern pictures, and still more for modern painters. To this Madame Peloux had replied: 'I believe in letting well alone.'

If the muddy green paint – 'The green of hospital corridors', Léa called it – flaked off in one of the passages, Madame Peloux would have it repainted a similar muddy green; or if the maroon velvet on a *chaise-longue* needed replacing, she was careful to choose the same maroon velvet.

Chéri paused by the open door of a dressing-room. Embedded in the maroon marble-topped wash-stand were jug and basin of plain white with a monogram, and over the two electric-light fittings were lily-shaped bead shades. Chéri shuddered as though caught in a violent draught – 'Good God, how hideous, what an old junk-shop!'

He hurried away. At the end of the passage, he came upon a window edged with small pieces of red and yellow stained glass. 'That's the last straw!' he said grumpily.

He turned to the left and roughly opened a door – the door of his nursery – without knocking. A little cry came from the bed where Edmée was just finishing her breakfast. Chéri closed the door and stared at his wife without going any closer.

'Good morning,' she said with a smile. 'You do look surprised to see me here!'

She lay bathed in a steady blue light reflected from the snow outside. Her crimped ashy chestnut hair was down, but barely covered her prettily curved shoulders. With her pink-and-white cheeks matching her nightgown, and her rosy lips paler than usual from fatigue, she looked like a light-toned picture, not quite finished and rather misty.

'Aren't you going to say good morning to me, Fred?' she insisted.

He sat down close beside his wife and took her in his arms. She fell back gently, dragging him with her. Chéri propped himself on his elbow to look down more closely at her. She was so young that even when tired she still looked fresh. He seemed astonished by the smoothness of her fully rounded lower eyelids, and by the silvery softness of her cheeks.

'How old are you?' he asked suddenly.

Edmée opened her eyes, which she had closed voluptuously. Chéri stared at the brown of their pupils and at her small square teeth.

'Oh, come! I shall be nineteen on the fifth of January, and do try and remember it.'

He drew his arm away roughly and the young woman slipped into the hollow of the bed like a discarded scarf.

'Nineteen, it's prodigious! Do you know that I'm over twenty-five?'

'But of course I know that, Fred. ...'

He picked up a pale tortoiseshell mirror from the bed-table and gazed at himself. 'Twenty-five years old!'

Twenty-five years of age and a face of white marble that seemed indestructible. Twenty-five, but at the outer corners of the eye and beneath it – delicately plagiarizing the classical design of the eyelid – were two lines, visible only in full light, two incisions traced by the lightest, the most relentless, of fingers.

He put back the mirror: 'You're younger than I am. That shocks me.'

'Not me!'

She had answered in a biting voice, full of hidden meaning. He took no notice.

'Do you know why my eyes are beautiful?' he asked in all seriousness.

'No,' Edmée said. 'Perhaps because I love them?'

'Stuff!' Chéri said, shrugging his shoulders. 'It's because they're shaped like a sole.'

'Like what?'

'Like a sole.'

He sat down near her to give a demonstration.

'Look – here – the corner next the nose is the head of the sole. And then – the upper curve, that's the back of the sole; whereas the lower line runs perfectly straight and that's its belly. And the other corner that tapers up to my temples, that's the sole's tail.'

53

'Oh?'

'Yes, but if I had an eye shaped like a flounder, that's to say, with the lower part as much curved as the top, then I should look silly. See? You've passed your matric., did you know that?'

'No, I must admit ...'

She broke off, feeling guilty, because he had spoken sententiously and with exaggerated passion, like someone with a mania. 'There are moments when he looks like a savage,' she thought, 'like a man from the jungle. Yet he knows nothing about plants or animals, and sometimes he doesn't seem even to know about human beings.'

Sitting close beside her, Chéri put one arm round her shoulders and with his free hand began to finger the small, evenly matched, very round and very beautiful, pearls of her necklace. Intoxicated by the scent which Chéri used too much of, she began to droop like a rose in an overheated room.

'Fred! Come back to sleep! We're both tired. ...'

He seemed not to have heard. He was staring at the pearls with obsessed anxiety.

'Fred?'

He shivered, leaped to his feet, furiously tore off his pyjamas and jumped naked into bed, seeking the place to rest his head on a shoulder where the delicate collar-bone was still youthfully sharp. The whole of Edmée's body obeyed his will as she opened her arms to him. Chéri closed his eyes and never moved. She took care to remain awake, a little smothered under his weight, and thinking him asleep. But almost at once he turned over away from her with a sudden pitch, imitating the groans of someone fast asleep, and rolled himself up in the sheet at the other side of the bed.

'He always does that,' Edmée noted.

All through the winter, she was to awaken in this square room with its four windows. Bad weather delayed the completion of the new house in the Avenue Henri-Martin – bad weather, and Chéri's whims. He wanted a black bathroom, a Chinese drawing-room, a basement fitted up with a swimming pool and gymnasium. To the architect's objections he would answer: 'I don't give a damn. I pay, I want the work done. To hell with the cost.' But every now and again he would cast a ruthless eye over an estimate and proclaim 'You can't bamboozle young Peloux.' Indeed, he held forth on standardization, fibro-cement, and coloured stucco with unexpected glibness and a memory for exact figures that compelled the contractor's respect.

Rarely did he consult his young wife, although he paraded his authority for her benefit and took pains, when occasion arose, to cover his deficiencies by giving curt commands. She was to find that he possessed an instinctive eye for colour, but had only contempt for beauty of shape and period differences.

'You simply clutter up your head with all that stuff and nonsense, what's your name, yes, you, Edmée. An idea for the smoking-room? All right, here's one: Blue for the walls — a ferocious blue. The carpet purple — a purple that plays second fiddle to the blue of the walls. Against that you needn't be afraid of using as much black as you like and a splash of gold in the furniture and ornaments.'

'Yes, you're right, Fred. But it will be rather drastic with all those strong colours. It's going to look rather charmless without a lighter note somewhere ... a white vase or a statue.'

'Nonsense,' he interrupted rather sharply. 'The white vase you want will be me — me, stark naked. And we mustn't forget a cushion or some thingumabob in pumpkin-red for when I'm running about stark naked in the smoking-room.'

Secretly attracted and at the same time disgusted, she cherished these fanciful ideas for turning their future home into a sort of disreputable palace, a temple to the greater glory of her husband. She offered little resistance, just gently requested 'some little corner' for a small and precious set of furniture upholstered with needlework on a white ground — a present from Marie-Laure.

This gentleness masked a determination that was young yet far from inexperienced; it stood her in good stead during the four months of camping out in her mother-in-law's house. It enabled her to evade, throughout these four months, the enemy stalking her, the traps laid daily to destroy her equanimity, her still susceptible gaiety, and her tact. Charlotte Peloux, over-excited at the proximity of so tender a victim, was inclined to lose her head and squander her barbs, using her claws indiscriminately.

'Keep calm, Madame Peloux,' Chéri would throw out from time to time. 'What bones will there be left for you to pick next winter if I don't stop you now?'

Edmée raised frightened, grateful eyes to her husband, and did her best not to think too much, not to look too much, at Madame Peloux. One evening Charlotte, almost heedlessly, three times tossed across the chrysanthemum table-piece Léa's name instead of Edmée's.

Chéri lowered his satanic eyebrows: 'Madame Peloux, I believe your memory is giving way. Perhaps a rest cure is indicated?'

Charlotte Peloux held her tongue for a whole week, but Edmée never dared to ask her husband: 'Did you get angry on my behalf? Was it me you were defending? Or was it that other woman, the one before me?'

Life as a child and then as a girl had taught her patience, hope, silence; and given her a prisoner's proficiency in handling these virtues as weapons. The fair Marie-Laure had never scolded her daughter: she had merely punished her. Never a hard word, never a tender one. Utter loneliness, then a boarding-school, then again loneliness in the holidays and frequent relegations to a bedroom. Finally, the threat of marriage – any marriage – from the moment that the eye of a too beautiful mother had discerned in the daughter the dawn of a rival beauty, shy, timid, looking a victim of tyranny, and all the more touching for that. In comparison with this inhuman gold-and-ivory mother, Charlotte Peloux and her spontaneous malice seemed a bed of roses.

'Are you frightened of my respected parent?' Chéri asked her one evening.

Edmée smiled and pouted to show her indifference: 'Frightened? No. You aren't frightened when a door slams, though it may make you jump. It's a snake creeping under it that's frightening.'

'A terrific snake, Marie-Laure, isn't she?'

'Terrific.'

He waited for confidences that did not come and put a brotherly arm round his wife's slender shoulders: 'We're sort of orphans, you and I, aren't we?'

'Yes, we're orphans, and we're so sweet!'

She clung to him. They were alone in the big sitting-room, for Madame Peloux was upstairs concocting, as Chéri put it, her poisons for the following day. The night was cold and the window panes reflected the lamplight and furnishings like a pond. Edmée felt warm and protected, safe in the arms of this unknown man. She lifted her head and gave a cry of alarm. He was staring up at the chandelier above them with a look of desperation on his magnificent features, and two tears hung glistening between the lids of his half-closed eyes.

'Chéri, Chéri, what's the matter with you?' On the spur of the moment she had called him by the too endearing nickname she had never meant to pronounce. He answered its appeal in bewilderment and turned his eyes down to look at her.

'Chéri, oh God! I'm frightened. What's wrong with you?'

He pushed her away a little, and held her facing him.

'Oh! Oh! You poor child, you poor little thing! What are you frightened of?'

He gazed at her with his eyes of velvet, wide-open, peaceful, inscrutable, all the more handsome for his tears. Edmée was about to beg him not to speak, when he said, 'How silly we are! It's the idea that we're orphans. It's idiotic. It's so true.'

He resumed his air of comic self-importance, and she drew a breath of relief, knowing that he would say no more. He began switching off all the lights with his usual care, and then turned to Edmée with a vanity that was either very simple or very deceitful: 'Well, why shouldn't I have a heart like everybody else?'

'WHAT are you doing there?'
He had called out to her almost in a whisper, yet the sound of Chéri's voice struck Edmée so forcibly that she swayed forward as if he had pushed her. She was standing beside a big open writing-desk and she spread her hands over the papers scattered in front of her.

'I'm tidying up ...' she said in a dazed voice. She lifted a hand and it remained poised in mid-air as though benumbed. Then she appeared to wake up, and stopped lying.

'It's like this, Fred. You told me that when we came to move house you'd hate to be bothered over what you'd want to take with you, all the things in this room ... the furniture. I honestly wanted to tidy, to sort things. Then the poison, temptation came ... evil thoughts ... one evil thought. ... I implore your forgiveness. I've touched things that don't belong to me. ...'

She trembled bravely and waited.

He stood with his forehead jutting forward, his hands clenched in a threatening attitude; but he did not seem to see his wife. His eyes were strangely veiled, and ever after she was to retain the impression of having spoken with a man whose eyes were deathly pale.

'Ah, yes,' he said at length. 'You were looking ... you were looking for love-letters.' She did not deny it. 'You were hunting for my love-letters.'

He laughed his awkward, constrained laugh.

Edmée felt hurt, and blushed. 'Of course you must think me a fool. As if you were the kind of man not to lock them away in a safe place or burn them! And then, anyhow, they're none of my business. I've only got what I deserved. You won't hold it too much against me, Fred?'

Her pleading had cost her a certain effort, and she tried deliberately to make herself look appealing, pouting her lips a little and keeping the upper half of her face shadowed by her fluffy hair. But Chéri did not relax his attitude, and she noticed for the first time that the unblemished skin of his cheeks had taken on the transparence of a white rose in winter, and that their oval contour had shrunk.

'Love-letters,' he repeated. 'That's howlingly funny.'

He took a step forward, seized a fistful of papers and scattered them: post-cards, restaurant bills, tradespeople's announcements, telegrams from chorus girls met one night and never seen again, *pneumatiques* of four or five lines from sponging friends; and several close-written pages slashed with the sabre-like script of Madame Peloux.

Chéri turned round again to his wife: 'I have no love-letters.'

'Oh!' she protested. 'Why do you want –'

'I have none,' he interrupted; 'you can never understand. I've never noticed it myself until now. I can't have any love-letters because –' He checked himself. 'But wait, wait. ... Yes, there was one occasion, I remember, when I didn't want to go to La Bourboule, and it ... Wait, wait.'

He began pulling out drawers and feverishly tossing papers to the floor.

'That's too bad! What can I have done with it? I could have sworn it was in the upper left-hand ... No. ...'

He slammed back the empty drawers and glowered at Edmée.

'You found nothing? You didn't take a letter which began "But what do you expect, I'm not in the least bored. There's nothing better than to be separated one week in every month," and then went on to something else. I don't remember what, something about honeysuckle climbing high enough to look in at the window.'

He broke off, simply because his memory refused to come to his aid, and he was left gesticulating in his impatience.

Slim and recalcitrant, Edmée did not quail before him. She took refuge in caustic irritability. 'No, no, I *took* nothing. Since when have I been capable of *taking* things? But if this letter is so very precious to you, how is it you've left it lying about? I've no need to inquire whether it was one of Léa's?'

He winced, but not quite in the manner Edmée had expected. The ghost of a smile hovered over his handsome, unresponsive features; and, with his head on one side, an expectant look in his eyes, and the delicious bow of his mouth taut-stretched, he might well have been listening to the echo of a name.

59

The full force of Edmée's young and ill-disciplined emotions burst forth in a series of sobs and tears, and her fingers writhed and twisted as if ready to scratch. 'Go away! I hate you! You've never loved me. I might not so much as exist, for all the notice you take of me! You hurt me, you despise me, you're insulting, you're, you're ... You think only of that old woman! It's not natural, it's degenerate, it's ... You don't love me! Why, oh why, did you ever marry me? ... You're ... you're ...'

She was tossing her head like an animal caught by the neck, and as she leaned back to take a deep breath, because she was suffocating, the light fell on her string of small, milky, evenly matched pearls. Chéri stared in stupefaction at the controlled movements of the lovely throat, at the hands clasped together in appeal, and above all at the tears, her tears. ... He had never seen such a torrent of tears. For who had ever wept in front of him, or wept because of him? No one. Madame Peloux? 'But', he thought, 'Madame Peloux's tears don't count.' Léa? No. Searching his memory, he appealed to a pair of honest blue eyes; but they had sparkled with pleasure only, or malice, or a rather mocking tenderness. Such floods of tears poured down the cheeks of this writhing young woman. What could be done about all these tears? He did not know. All the same, he stretched out an arm, and as Edmée drew back, fearing some brutality perhaps, he placed his beautiful, gentle, scented hand on her head and patted her ruffled hair. He did his best to copy the tone and speech of a voice whose power he knew so well: 'There, there. ... What's it all about? What's the matter, then? There ... there. ...'

Edmée collapsed suddenly, fell back huddled in a heap on a settee, and broke out into frenzied and passionate sobbing that sounded like yells of laughter or howls of joy. As she lay doubled up, her graceful body heaved and rocked with grief, jealousy, fury, and an unsuspected servility. And yet, like a wrestler in the heat of a struggle, or a swimmer in the hollow of a wave, she felt bathed in some strange new atmosphere, both natural and harsh.

She had a good long cry, and recovered by slow degrees, with periods of calm shaken by great shudders and gasps for breath. Chéri sat down by her side and continued to stroke her hair. The crisis of his own emotion was over, and he felt bored. He ran his eyes over Edmée as she lay sideways upon the unyielding settee. This straggling body, with its rucked-up frock and trailing scarf, added to the disorder of the room; and this displeased him.

Soft as was his sigh of boredom, she heard it and sat up. 'Yes,' she said, 'I'm more than you can stand. ... Oh! it would be better to ...'

He interrupted her, fearing a torrent of words: 'It's not that. It's simply that I don't know what you want.'

'What I want? How d'you mean, what I ...'

She lifted her face, still wet with tears.

'Now listen to me.' He took her hands.

She tried to free herself. 'No, no, I know that tone of voice. You're going to treat me to another of those nonsensical outbursts. When you put on that tone of voice and face, I know you're going to prove that your eye is shaped like a striped super-mullet, or that your mouth looks like the figure three on its side. No, no, I can't stand that!'

Her recriminations were childish, and Chéri relaxed, feeling that after all they were both very young. He pressed her warm hands between his own.

'But you must listen to me! ... Good God! I'd like to know what you've got to reproach me with! Do I ever go out in the evenings without you? No! Do I often leave you on your own during the day? Do I carry on a secret correspondence?'

'I don't know – I don't think so –'

He turned her this way and that like a doll.

'Do I have a separate room? Don't I make love to you well?'

She hesitated, smiling with exquisite suspicion. 'Do you call that love, Fred?'

'There are other words for it, but you wouldn't appreciate them.'

'What you call love ... isn't it possible that it may be, really, a ... kind ... of alibi?' She hastened to add, 'I'm merely generalizing, Fred, of course ... I said "*may be*", in certain cases. ...'

He dropped Edmée's hands. 'That', he said coldly, 'is putting your foot right in it.'

'Why?' she asked in a feeble voice.

He whistled, chin in air, as he moved back a step or two. Then he advanced upon his wife, looking her up and down as if she were a stranger. To instil fear a fierce animal has no need to leap. Edmée noticed that his nostrils were dilating and that the tip of his nose was white.

'Ugh!' he breathed, looking at his wife. He shrugged his shoulders, turned, and walked away. At the end of the room he turned round and came back again. 'Ugh!' he repeated. 'Look what's talking!'

'What are you saying?'

'Look what's talking, and what it says. Upon my word, it actually has the cheek to ...'

She jumped up in a rage. 'Fred,' she said, 'don't dare to speak to me again in that tone! What do you take me for?'

'For a woman who knows exactly how to put her foot in it, as I've just had the honour of informing you.'

He touched her on the shoulder with a rigid forefinger, and this hurt her as much as if he had inflicted a serious bruise. 'You've matriculated; isn't there somewhere some kind of a proverb which says "Never play with knives or daggers" or whatever it may be?'

'Cold steel,' she answered automatically.

'That's right. Well, my child, you must never play with cold steel. That's to say, you must never be wounding about a man's ... a man's favours, if I may so express it. You were wounding about the gifts, about the favours, I bestow on you.'

'You ... you talk like a cocotte,' she gasped.

She blushed, and her strength and self-control deserted her. She hated him for remaining cool and collected, for keeping his superiority: its whole secret lay in the carriage of his head, the sureness of his stance, the poise of his arms and shoulders.

The hard forefinger once more pressed into Edmée's shoulder.

'Excuse me, excuse me ... It'll probably come as a great surprise when I state that, on the contrary, it's you who have the mentality of a tart. When it comes to judging such matters, there's no greater authority than young Peloux. I'm a connoisseur of "cocottes", as you call them. I know them inside out. A "cocotte" is a lady who generally manages to receive more than she gives. Do you hear what I say?'

What she heard above all was that he was now addressing her like a stray acquaintance.

'Nineteen years old, white skin, hair that smells of vanilla; and then, in bed, closed eyes and limp arms. That's all very pretty, but is there anything unusual about it? Do you really think it so very unusual?'

She had started at each word, and each sting had goaded her towards the duel of female versus male.

'It may be very unusual,' she said in a steady voice, 'how could *you* know?'

He did not answer, and she hastened to take advantage of a hit. 'Personally, I saw much handsomer men than you when we were in Italy. The streets were full of them. My nineteen years are worth those of any other girl of my age, just as one good-looking man is as good as the next. Don't worry, everything can be arranged. Nowadays, marriage is not an important undertaking. Instead of allowing silly scenes to make us bitter …'

He put a stop to what she had to say by an almost pitying shake of the head.

'My poor kid, it's not so simple as that.'

'Why not? There's such a thing as quick divorce, if one's ready to pay.'

She spoke in the peremptory manner of a runaway schoolgirl, and it was pathetic. She had pushed back the hair off her forehead, and her anxious, intelligent eyes were made to look all the darker by the soft contours of her cheeks now fringed with hair: the eyes of an unhappy woman, eyes mature and definitive in a still undeveloped face.

'That wouldn't help at all,' Chéri said.

'Because?'

'Because …' He leaned forward with his eyelashes tapered into pointed wings, shut his eyes and opened them again as if he had just swallowed a bitter pill. 'Because you love me.'

She noticed that he had resumed the more familiar form of addressing her, and above all the fuller, rather choked tones of their happiest hours. In her heart of hearts she acquiesced: 'It's true, I love him. At the moment, there's no remedy.'

The dinner bell sounded in the garden – a bell which was too small, dating from before Madame Peloux's time, a sad clear bell reminiscent of a country orphanage. Edmée shivered. 'Oh, I don't like that bell. ...'

'No?' said Chéri, absent-mindedly.

'In our house, dinner will be announced. There'll be no bell. There'll be no boarding-house habits in our home – you'll see.'

She spoke these words without turning round, while walking down the hospital-green corridor, and so did not see, behind her, either the fierce attention Chéri paid to her last words, or his silent laughter.

HE was walking along with a light step, stimulated by the rathe spring, perceptible in the moist gusty wind and the exciting earthy smells of squares and private gardens. Every now and again a fleeting glimpse in a glass would remind him that he was wearing a becoming felt hat, pulled down over the right eye, a loose-fitting spring coat, large light-coloured gloves, and a terra-cotta tie. The eyes of women followed his progress with silent homage, the more candid among them bestowing that passing stupe-faction which can be neither feigned nor hidden. But Chéri never looked at women in the street. He had just come from his house in the Avenue Henri-Martin, having left various orders with the up-holsterers: orders contradicting one another, but thrown out in a tone of authority.

On reaching the end of the Avenue, he took a deep breath of the good spring scents carried up from the Bois on the heavy moist wing of the west wind, and then hurried on his way to the Porte Dauphine. Within a few minutes he had reached the lower end of the Avenue Bugeaud, and there he stopped. For the first time in six months his feet were treading the familiar road. He unbuttoned his coat.

'I've been walking too fast,' he said to himself. He started off again, then paused and, this time, trained his eyes on one particular spot: fifty yards or so down the road – bareheaded, shammy-leather in hand, Ernest the concierge – Léa's concierge – was 'doing' the brasswork of the railings in front of Léa's house. Chéri began to hum, realized from the sound of his voice that he never did hum, and stopped.

'How are things, Ernest? Hard at work as usual?'

The concierge brightened respectfully.

'Monsieur Peloux! It's a pleasure to see Monsieur again. Monsieur has not changed at all.'

'Neither have you, Ernest. Madame is well, I hope?'

He turned his head away to gaze up at the closed shutters on the first floor.

'I expect so, Monsieur, all we've had has been a few post-cards.'

'Where from? Was it Biarritz?'

'I don't think so, Monsieur.'

'Where is Madame?'

'It wouldn't be easy for me to tell you, Monsieur. We forward all letters addressed to Madame – and there's none to speak of – to Madame's solicitor.'

Chéri pulled out his note-case, and cocked an eye at Ernest.

'Oh, Monsieur Peloux, money between you and me? Don't think of it. A thousand francs won't make a man tell what he doesn't know. But if Monsieur would like the address of Madame's solicitor?'

'No thanks, there's no point. And when does she return?'

Ernest threw up his hands: 'That's another question that's beyond me. Maybe tomorrow, maybe in a month's time. ... I keep every-thing in readiness, just the same. You have to watch out where Madame is concerned. If you said to me now, "There she comes round the corner of the Avenue," I shouldn't be surprised.'

Chéri turned round and looked towards the corner of the Avenue.

'That's all Monsieur Peloux wants? Monsieur just happened to be walking by? It's a lovely day. ...'

'Nothing else, thank you, Ernest. Goodbye, Ernest.'

'Always at Monsieur's service.'

Chéri walked up as far as the Place Victor-Hugo, swinging his cane as he went. Twice he stumbled and almost fell, like people who imagine their progress is being followed by hostile eyes. On reaching the balustraded entrance to the Métro, he leaned over the ramp to peer down into the pink-and-black recesses of the Underground, and felt utterly exhausted. When he straightened his back, he saw that the lamps had been lighted in the square and that the blue of dusk coloured everything around him.

'No, it can't be true. I'm ill.'

He had plumbed the depths of cavernous memories and his re-turn to the living world was painful. The right words came to him at last. 'Pull yourself together, Peloux, for God's sake! Are you losing your head, my boy? Don't you know it's time to go back home?'

This last word recalled a sight that one hour had sufficed to banish from his mind: a large square room – his own nursery; an anxious young woman standing by the window; and Charlotte Peloux, subdued by a Martini.

'Oh, no,' he said aloud. 'Not that! That's all over.'

He signalled to a taxi with his raised stick.

'To the ... er ... to the Restaurant du Dragon Bleu.'

Chéri crossed the grill-room to the sound of violins in the glare of the atrocious electric light, and this had a tonic effect. He shook the hand of a maître d'hôtel who recognized him. Before him rose the stooping figure of a tall young man. Chéri gave an affectionate gasp. 'Desmond, the very man I wanted to see! Howdydo?'

They were shown to a table decorated with pink carnations. A small hand and a towering aigrette beckoned towards Chéri from a neighbouring table.

'It's La Loupiote,' Vicomte Desmond warned him.

Chéri had no recollection of La Loupiote, but he smiled towards the towering aigrette and, without getting up, touched the small hand with a paper fan lying on his table. Then he put on his most solemn 'conquering hero' look, and swept his eyes over an unknown couple. The woman had forgotten to eat since he had sat down in her vicinity.

'The man with her looks a regular cuckold, doesn't he?'

He had leaned over to whisper into his friend's ear, and his eyes shone with pleasure as if with rising tears.

'What d'you drink, now you're married?' Desmond asked. 'Camomile tea?'

'Pommery,' Chéri said.

'And before the Pommery?'

'Pommery, before and after.' And, dilating his nostrils, he sniffed as he remembered some sparkling, rose-scented old champagne of 1889 that Léa kept for him alone.

He ordered a meal that a shopgirl out on the spree might choose – cold fish *au porto*, a roast bird, and a piping hot soufflé which concealed in its innards a red ice, sharp on the tongue.

'Hullo!' La Loupiote shouted, waving a pink carnation at Chéri.

'Hullo,' Chéri answered, raising his glass.

The chimes of an English wall-clock struck eight. 'Blast!' Chéri grumbled. 'Desmond, go and make a telephone call for me.'

Desmond's pale eyes were hungry for revelations to come.

'Go and ask for Wagram 17-08, tell them to put you through to my mother, and say we're dining together.'

'And supposing young Madame Peloux comes to the telephone?'

'Say the same thing. I'm not tied to her apron-strings. I've got her well trained.'

He ate and drank a lot, taking the greatest care to appear serious and blasé; but his pleasure was enhanced by the least sound of laughter, the clink of glasses, or the strains of a syrupy valse. The steely blue of the highly glazed woodwork reminded him of the Riviera, at the hour when the too blue sea grows dark around the blurred reflection of the noonday sun. He forgot that very handsome young men ought to pretend indifference; he began to scrutinize the dark girl opposite, so that she trembled all over under his expert gaze.

'What about Léa?' Desmond asked suddenly.

Chéri did not jump: he was thinking of Léa. 'Léa? She's in the south.'

'Is all over between you?'

Chéri put his thumb in the armhole of his waistcoat.

'Well, of course, what d'you expect? We parted in proper style, the best of friends. It couldn't last a lifetime. What a charming, intelligent woman, old man! But then, you know her yourself! Broadminded ... most remarkable. My dear fellow, I confess that if it hadn't been for the question of age ... But there *was* the question of age, and you agree –'

'Of course,' Desmond interrupted.

This young man with lack-lustre eyes, though he knew just how to perform the wearing and difficult duties of a parasite, had just yielded to curiosity and blamed himself for such rashness. Chéri, circumspect and at the same time highly elated, never stopped talking about Léa. He made all the right remarks, showed all the sound sense of a married man. He spoke in praise of marriage, while giving Léa's virtues their due. He extolled the submissive sweetness of his young wife, and thus found occasion to criticize Léa's independence of character. 'Oh, the old devil, she had her own ideas about everything, I can tell you!'

He went a step further in his confidences, speaking of Léa with severity, and even impertinence. He was sheltering behind idiotic words, prompted by the suspicions of a deceived lover, and at the same time enjoying the subtle pleasure of being able to speak of her without danger. A little more, and he would have sullied her name, while his heart was rejoicing in his own memories of her: sullied the soft sweet name which he had been unable to mention freely during the last six months, and the whole gracious vision he had of Léa, leaning over him with her two or three irreparable wrinkles, and her beauty, now lost to him, but – alas – ever present.

About eleven o'clock they rose to go, chilled by the emptiness of the almost deserted restaurant. However, at the next table, La Loupiote was busy writing letters and had called for telegraph forms. She raised her white, inoffensive, sheeplike head as the two friends passed by. 'Well, aren't you even going to say good evening?'

'Good evening,' Chéri condescended to say.

La Loupiote drew her friend's attention to Chéri's good looks. 'Would you believe it! And to think that he's got such pots of money. Some people have everything!'

But when Chéri merely offered her an open cigarette-case, she became vituperative. 'They have everything, except the knowledge of how to make proper use of it. Go back home to your mother, dearie!'

'Look here,' Chéri said to Desmond when they were outside in the narrow street. 'Look here, I was about to ask you, Desmond ... Wait till we get away from this beastly crowd. ...'

The soft damp evening air had kept people lingering in the streets, but the theatre-goers from the Rue Caumartin onwards had not yet packed the Boulevard. Chéri took his friend by the arm: 'Look here, Desmond ... I wanted you to make another telephone call.'

Desmond stopped, 'Again?'

'You'll ask for Wagram–'

'17–08.'

'You're marvellous ... Say that I've been taken ill in your flat. Where are you living?'

'Hôtel Morris.'

'Splendid – and that I won't be back till morning, and that you're making me some mint tea. Go on, old man. Here, you can give this to the telephone-girl, or else keep it yourself. But come back quickly. I'll be sitting waiting for you outside Weber's.'

The tall young man, arrogant and serviceable, went off crumpling the franc-notes in his pocket, without permitting himself a comment. When Desmond rejoined him, Chéri was slouched over an untouched orangeade in which he appeared to be reading his fortune.

'Desmond ... Who answered you?'

'A lady,' the laconic messenger replied.

'Which?'

'Dunno.'

'What did she say?'

'That it was all right.'

'In what tone of voice?'

'Same as I'm speaking to you in.'

'Oh, good. Thanks.'

'It was Edmée,' thought Chéri.

They were walking towards the Place de la Concorde and Chéri linked arms with Desmond. He did not dare to admit that he was feeling dog-tired.

'Where do you want to go?' Desmond asked.

'Well, old man,' Chéri sighed in gratitude, 'to the Morris; and as soon as we can. I'm fagged out.'

Desmond forgot to be impassive. 'What? It can't be true. To the Morris? What d'you want to do? No nonsense! D'you want to ...'

'To go to bed,' Chéri answered. And he closed his eyes as though on the point of dropping off, then opened them again. 'Sleep, I want to sleep, got it?'

He gripped his friend's arm too hard.

'Let's go there, then,' Desmond said.

Within ten minutes they were at the Morris. The sky-blue and white bedroom and the imitation Empire furniture of the sitting-room smiled at Chéri like old friends. He took a bath, borrowed one of Desmond's silk night-shirts which was too tight for him, got into bed, and, wedged between two huge soft pillows, sank into dreamless bliss, into the dark depths of a sleep that protected him from all attacks.

H E began to count the shameful days as they went by. 'Sixteen ... seventeen ... When three weeks are up, I'll go back to Neuilly.' He did not go back. Though he saw the situation quite clearly, he no longer had the strength to cure it. At night, and in the morning sometimes, he flattered himself that he would get over his cowardice within an hour or two. 'No strength left? ... Please, please, I beg of you ... Not yet strength enough. But it's coming back. What's the betting I'll be in the Boulevard d'Inkermann dining-room at the stroke of twelve? One, two ...' The stroke of twelve found him in the bath, or else driving his motor, with Desmond at his side.

At every meal-time he felt optimistic for a moment about his marriage. This feeling was as regular as a recurrent fever. As he sat down facing Desmond at their bachelor table, the ghost of Edmée would appear, and plunge him into silent thoughts of his young wife's inconceivable deference. 'Really, that young thing's too sweet! Did you ever see such a dream of a wife? Never a word, never a complaint! I'll treat her to one of those bracelets when I get back. ... Upbringing, that's what does it! Give me Marie-Laure every time for bringing up a daughter!' But one day in the grill-room at the Morris, abject terror was written on his face when he caught sight of a green dress with a chinchilla collar just like one of Edmée's dresses.

Desmond found life wonderful and was getting a little fat. He reserved his arrogance for moments when Chéri – encouraged by him to pay a visit to some 'prodigious English girl, riddled with vice', or to some 'Indian potentate in his opium palace' – refused point-blank or else consented with unconcealed scorn. Desmond had long since despaired of understanding Chéri's ways; but Chéri was paying – and better than during the best of their bachelor days to-gether. They ran across the blonde La Loupiote a second time, when they visited a friend of hers, a woman who boasted such an ordinary name that nobody ever remembered it; 'What's-her-name ... you know perfectly well ... that pal of La Loupiote's.'

The Pal smoked opium, and gave it to others. The instant you came into her modest, ground-floor flat, you smelt escaping gas and stale drugs. She won the hearts of her guests by a tearful cordiality and by a constant incitement to self-pity – both objectionable traits. She treated Desmond, when he paid her a visit, as 'a great big desperately lonesome boy', ... and Chéri as 'a beauty who has got everything and it only makes him more miserable'. Chéri never touched the pipe; he looked at the small box of cocaine with the repugnance of a cat about to be dosed, and spent most of the night with his back against the cushioned dado, sitting up on a straw mat between Desmond, who went to sleep, and the Pal, who never stopped smoking. For most of the night he breathed in the fumes that satisfy all hunger and thirst, but his self-control and distrust persisted. He appeared to be perfectly happy, except that he stared now and then, with pained and questioning intensity, at the Pal's withered throat – a skinny, far too red throat, round which shimmered a string of false pearls.

Once, he stretched out a hand and with the tip of his fingers touched the henna-tinted hair on the nape of her neck. He judged the weight of the big light hollow pearls with his hand, then snatched it back with the nervous shiver of someone who catches his finger-nail on a piece of frayed silk. Not long after, he got up and went.

'Aren't you sick to death of all this,' Desmond asked Chéri, 'sick of these poky holes where we eat and drink and never have any girls? Sick of this hotel with the doors always slamming? Sick of the night clubs where we go in the evenings, and of dashing in that fast car of yours from Paris to Rouen, Paris to Compiègne, Paris to Ville d'Avray? ... Why not the Riviera for a change? The season down there isn't December and January, it's March, April, or – '

'No,' said Chéri.

'Then what?'

'Then nothing.'

Chéri affected to become amiable and put on what Léa used to call 'his air of worldly superiority'.

'Dear old boy ... you don't seem to appreciate the beauty of Paris at this time of the year. ... This ... er ... indecisive season, this spring that doesn't seem willing to smile, the softness of the light ... as opposed to the commonplace Riviera. ... No, don't you see, I like it here.'

Desmond all but lost his lackey patience. 'Yes, and besides, it may be that the young Peloux's divorce will ...'

Chéri's sensitive nostrils blenched. 'If you've arranged to touch a commission from some lawyer friend, you can drop the idea at once. There'll be no such thing as "young Peloux's divorce".'

'My dear fellow! ...' Desmond protested, doing his best to look hurt. 'You have a very curious way of behaving to a man who has been a friend since your childhood, and who has always ...'

Chéri was not listening. Instead, he pushed towards Desmond's face a pointed chin and a mouth pursed like a miser's. For the first time in his life he had heard a stranger disposing of his possessions.

He began to reflect. Young Peloux's divorce? Many nights and days had he spent in thinking over these words till they had come to spell liberty, a sort of second boyhood, perhaps something even better. But Desmond's voice, with its affected nasal twang, had just called up the image he had been looking for: Edmée, resolute in her little hat with its long motoring veil, moving out of the house at Neuilly on her way to an unknown house to join an unknown man. 'Of course, that would settle everything,' and his Bohemian side was delighted. At the same time a surprisingly timorous Chéri jibbed, 'That's not the sort of way one behaves!' The image became focused in sharper colour and movement. Chéri could hear the heavy musical note of the iron gate swinging to, and could see beyond it fingers wearing a grey pearl and a white diamond. 'Farewell,' the small hand said.

Chéri jumped up, pushing back his seat. 'Those are mine, all of them! The woman, the house, the rings ... they all belong to me!'

He had not spoken out loud, but his features expressed such savage violence that Desmond thought his last hour of prosperity had struck. Chéri spoke to him pityingly but without kindness.

'Poor pussy-cat, did I scare you? What it is to be descended from the Crusaders! Come along, and I'll buy you pants as fine as my

74

shirts, and shirts as fine as your pants. Desmond, is today the seventeenth?'

'Yes, why?'

'The seventeenth of March. In other words, spring. Desmond, people who think themselves smart, I mean those in the height of fashion, women or men – can they afford to wait any longer before buying their spring wardrobes?'

'Hardly –'

'The seventeenth, Desmond! Come along at once; everything's all right. We're going to buy a huge bracelet for my wife, an enormous cigarette-holder for Madame Peloux, and a tiny tie-pin for you.'

On more than one such occasion he had felt an overwhelming presentiment that Léa was on the point of returning; that she was already back in her house; that the first-floor shutters had been opened, allowing a glimpse of the flowered pink net curtains across the windows, the lace of the full-length curtains at each side, and the glint of the looking-glasses. ... The fifteenth of April went by and still there was no sign of Léa.

The mournful monotony of Chéri's existence was tempered by several provoking incidents. There was a visit from Madame Peloux, who thought she was breathing her last when she found Chéri looking as thin as a greyhound, eyes wandering, and mouth tight shut. There was the letter from Edmée: a letter all in the same surprising tone, explaining that she would stay on at Neuilly 'until further orders', and had undertaken to pass on to Chéri 'Madame de la Berche's best regards'. ... He thought she was laughing at him, did not know what to answer, and ended by throwing away the enigmatic screed; but he did not go to Neuilly.

April advanced, leafy, cold, bright, and scenting all Paris with tulips, bunches of hyacinths, pawlonias, and laburnums like dropping-wells of gold. Chéri buried himself all the deeper in austere seclusion. The harassed, ill-treated, angry but well-paid Vicomte Desmond was given his orders: now to protect Chéri from familiar young women and indiscreet young men; now to recruit both sections and form a troop, who ate, drank, and rushed screaming at the top of their voices between Montmartre, the restaurants in the Bois, and the cabarets on the left bank.

One night the Pal was alone in her room, smoking opium and bewailing some shocking disloyalty of La Loupiote's, when her door opened to reveal the young man, with satanic eyebrows tapering towards his temples. He begged for 'a glass of really cold water' to allay some secret ardour that had parched his beautiful lips. He showed not the slightest interest in the Pal and the woes she poured out. She pushed towards him the lacquer tray with its pipe: he would accept nothing, and took up his usual position on the mat, to share with her the semi-obscurity in silence. There he stayed till dawn, moving as little as possible, like a man who fears that the least gesture may bring back his pain. At dawn, he questioned the Pal: 'Why weren't you wearing your pearls today; you know, the big ones?' and politely took his leave.

Walking alone at night was becoming an unconscious habit with him. With rapid lengthy strides he would make off towards some positive but inaccessible goal. Soon after midnight he would escape from Desmond, who discovered him again only towards daybreak, asleep on his hotel bed, flat on his stomach, his head pillowed on his folded arms, in the posture of a fretful child.

'Oh, good, he's here all right,' Desmond would say with relief. 'One can never be sure with such a crackpot.'

One night, when out on a tramp, his eyes wide open in the darkness, Chéri had felt compelled to walk up the Avenue Bugeaud; for during the day he had disregarded the superstition that made him return there once every twenty-four hours. There are maniacs who cannot go to sleep without having first touched the door-knob three times; a similar obsession made him run his hand along the railings, then put his finger to the bell-push, and call out Hullo! under his breath, as if in fun, before making off in haste.

But one night, that very night, as he stood before the railings, his heart jumped almost into his mouth: there, in the court, the electric globe shone like a mauve moon above the front-door steps, the back door stood wide open shedding a glow on the paved courtyard, while, on the first floor, the bedroom lights filtered through the shutters to make a golden comb. Chéri supported himself against the nearest tree and lowered his head.

'It can't be true. As soon as I look up, it will all be dark again.'

He straightened up at the sound of a voice. Ernest, the concierge, was shouting in the passage: 'At nine tomorrow, Marcel will help me carry up the big black trunk, Madame.'

Chéri turned round in a flash and ran as far as the Avenue du Bois. There he sat down. In front of his eyes danced the image of the electric globe he had been staring at – a dark purple ball fringed with gold, against a black group of trees in bud. He pressed his hand to his heart, and took a deep breath. Early lilac blossom scented the night air. He threw his hat away, undid the buttons of his overcoat, and, leaning back on a seat, let himself go, his legs outstretched and his hands hanging feebly by his sides. A crushing yet delicious weight had just fallen upon him. 'Ah!' he whispered, 'so this is what they call happiness. I never knew.'

For a moment he gave way to self-pity and self-contempt. How many good things had he missed by leading such a pointless life – a young man with lots of money and little heart! Then he stopped thinking for a moment, or possibly for an hour. Next, he persuaded himself there was nothing in the world he wanted, not even to go and see Léa.

When he found himself shivering in the cold, and heard the black-birds carolling the dawn, he got up and, stumbling a little but light-hearted, set off towards the Hôtel Morris without passing through the Avenue Bugeaud. He stretched himself, filled his lungs with the morning air, and overflowed with goodwill to all.

'Now,' he sighed, the devil driven out of him, 'now ... Oh now you'll see just how nice to the girl I shall be.'

Shaved, shod, and impatient – he had been up since eight – Chéri shook Desmond. Sleep gave him a swollen look, livid and quite frightful, like a drowned man. 'Desmond! Hey, Desmond! Up you get. ... You look too hideous when you're asleep!'

The sleeper woke, sat up, and turned towards Chéri eyes the colour of clouded water. He pretended to be fuddled with sleep so that he could make a long and close examination of Chéri – Chéri dressed in blue, pathetic, superb, and pale under the lightest coat of powder.

There were still moments when Desmond felt painfully aware of the contrast between his ugly mask and Chéri's good looks. He pretended to give a long yawn. 'What's he up to now?' he wondered. 'The idiot is in far better looks than yesterday – especially his eyelashes, and what eyelashes he has. ...' He was staring at the lustrous sweep of Chéri's thick lashes and the shadow they shed on the dark pupils and bluish whites of his eyes. Desmond noticed also that, this morning, the contemptuously arched lips were moist and fresh, and that he was breathing through them as if he had just that moment finished making love.

Quickly he relegated his jealousy to the back of his mind – where he kept his personal feelings – and asked Chéri in tones of weary condescension: 'May one inquire whether you are going out at this hour of the morning, or just coming in?'

'I'm going out,' Chéri said. 'Don't worry about me. I'm off shopping. I'm going to the florist's, the jeweller's, to my mother's, to my wife's, to ...'

'Don't forget the Papal Nuncio!'

'I know what's what,' Chéri answered. 'He shall have some imitation gold studs and a sheaf of orchids.'

It was rare for Chéri to respond to jokes: he usually accepted them in stony silence. His facetious reply proved that he was pleased with himself, and revealed this unaccustomed mood to Desmond. He studied Chéri's reflection in the looking-glass, noted the pallor of his dilated nostrils, observed that his eyes were continually on the rove, and ventured to put the most discreet of questions.

'Will you be coming back for luncheon? ... Hey, Chéri, I'm speaking to you. Are we lunching together?'

Chéri answered by shaking his head. He whistled softly, arranging himself in front of the pier-glass so that it framed his figure exactly like the one between the two windows in Léa's room – the one which would soon frame in its heavy gold, against a sunny pink background, the reflection of his body – naked or loosely draped in silk – the magnificent picture of a young man, handsome, loved, happy, and pampered, playing with the rings and necklaces of his mistress. 'Perhaps her young man's reflection is already there, in Léa's looking-glass!' This sudden thought cut so fiercely into his exhilaration that it dazed him, and he fancied he had heard it actually spoken.

'What did you say?' he asked Desmond.

'I never said a word,' his well-trained friend said stiffly. 'It must have been someone talking outside in the courtyard.'

Chéri went out, slamming the door behind him, and returned to his own rooms. They were filled with the dim continual hubbub of the fully awakened Rue de Rivoli, and Chéri, through the open window, could see the spring foliage, the leaves stiff and transparent like thin jade knives against the sun. He closed the window and sat down on a useless little chair which stood against the wall in a dingy corner between his bed and the bathroom door.

'How can it be? ...' he began in a low voice, and then said no more. He did not understand why it was that during the last six and a half months he had hardly given a thought to Léa's lover. '*I'm making a perfect fool of myself,*' were the actual words of the letter so piously preserved by Charlotte Peloux.

'A perfect fool?' Chéri shook his head. 'It's funny, but that's not how I see her at all. What sort of a man can she be in love with? Somebody like Patron – rather than like Desmond, of course. An oily little Argentine? Maybe. Yet all the same ...' He smiled a simple smile. 'Apart from me, who is there she could possibly care for?'

A cloud passed over the sun and the room darkened. Chéri leaned his head against the wall. 'My Nounoune ... My Nounoune ... Have you betrayed me? Are you beastly enough to deceive me? ... Have you really done that?'

He tried to give a sharper edge to his suffering by a misuse of his imagination: the words and sights it presented left him more astonished than enraged. He did his best to evoke the elation of early morning delights when he was living with Léa, the solace of the prolonged and perfect silences of certain afternoons, with Léa – the delicious sleepy hours in winter spent in a warm bed in a freshly aired room, with Léa ...; but, all the time, in the suffused cherry-coloured afternoon light aflame behind the curtains of Léa's room, he saw in Léa's arms one lover and one lover only – Chéri. He jumped up, revived by a spontaneous act of faith. 'It's as simple as that! If

79

I'm unable to see anyone but myself beside her, then it's because there is no one else to see.'

He seized the telephone, and was on the point of ringing her up, when he gently replaced the receiver. 'No nonsense. ....'

He walked out into the street, erect, with shoulders squared. He went in his open motor to the jeweller's, where he became sentimental over a slender little bandeau of burning blue sapphires invisibly mounted on blue steel, 'so exactly right for Edmée's hair', and took it away with him. He bought some stupid, rather pompous flowers. As it had only just struck eleven, he frittered away a further half-hour, drawing money from the Bank, turning over English illus-trated papers at a kiosk, visiting his scent-shop and a tobacconist's that specialized in Oriental cigarettes. Finally, he got back into his motor, and sat down between his sheaf of flowers and a heap of little beribboned parcels.

'Home.'

The chauffeur swivelled round on his basket-seat.

'Monsieur? ... What did Monsieur say? ...'

'I said Home – Boulevard d'Inkermann. D'you require a map of Paris?'

The motor went full speed towards the Champs-Élysées. The chauffeur drove much faster than usual and his thoughts could almost be read in his back. He seemed to be brooding uneasily over the gulf which divided the flabby young man of the past months – with his 'As you like', and his 'Have a glass of something, Antonin?' – from young Monsieur Peloux, strict with the staff and mindful of the petrol.

'Young Monsieur Peloux' leaned back against the morocco leather, hat on knees, drinking in the breeze and exerting all his energy in an effort not to think. Like a coward, he closed his eyes between the Avenue Malakoff and the Porte Dauphine to avoid a passing glimpse of the Avenue Bugeaud, and he congratulated himself on his resolution.

The chauffeur sounded his horn in the Boulevard d'Inkermann for the gate to be opened, and it sang on its hinges with a heavy musical note. The capped concierge hurried about his business, the watch-dogs barked in recognition of their returning master. Very much at his ease, sniffing the green smell of the newly mown lawns, Chéri entered the house and with a master's step climbed the stairs to the young woman whom he had left behind three months before, much as a sailor from Europe leaves behind, on the other side of the world, a little savage bride.

LÉA sat at her bureau, throwing away photographs from the last trunk to be unpacked. 'Heavens, how hideous people are! The women who had the nerve to give me these! And they think I'm going to put them up in a row on the mantelpiece – in plated frames or little folding-cases. Tear them all up quick, and straight into the waste-paper basket!'

She picked up the photographs again and, before throwing them away, subjected each to the closest scrutiny of which her blue eyes were capable. A postcard with a dark background of a powerful lady encased in full-length stays, doing her best to veil her hair and the lower part of her face with a wisp of tulle, in the teeth of a strong sea-breeze. '*To dearest Léa, in memory of exquisite hours spent at Guéthary. Anita.*' Another photograph, stuck on the middle of a piece of cardboard with a surface like dried mud, portrayed a large and lugubrious family. They might have been a penal colony, with a dumpy, heavily painted grandmother in charge. Holding above her head a tambourine tricked out with favours, she was resting one foot on the bent knee of what looked like a robust and shifty young butcher-boy. 'That should never have seen the light of day,' Léa said decisively, crumpling the rough-cast cardboard.

She smoothed out an unmounted print, to disclose two old provincial spinsters. An eccentric, loud-voiced, and aggressive couple, they were to be found every morning on a bench somewhere along a promenade, and every evening between a glass of cassis and their needlework-frames, on which they were embroidering black pussy-cats, fat toads, or a spider. '*To our beautiful fairy! From her little friends at Le Trayas, Miquette and Riquette.*'

Léa destroyed these souvenirs of her travels – and brushed a hand across her forehead. 'It's horrible. And there'll be dozens and dozens more after these, just as there were dozens before them, all much the same. There's nothing to be done about it. It's life. Maybe wherever a Léa is to be found, there at once spring from the earth a myriad creatures like Charlotte Peloux, de la Berche, and Aldonza, or old horrors who were once handsome young men, people who are ... well, who are impossible, impossible, impossible. ...'

She heard, so fresh was her memory, voices that had called out to her from the top of hotel steps or hailed her with a 'Hoo-hoo' from afar, across golden sands, and she lowered her head in anger like a bull.

She had returned, after an absence of six months, thinner, more flabby, less serene. Now and again a nervous twitch of the jaw jerked her chin down against her neck, and careless henna-shampoo-ing had left too orange a glint in her hair, but her skin had been tanned to amber by sea and wind. This gave her the glowing complexion of a handsome farmer's wife, and she might have done without rouge. All the same, she would have to arrange something carefully round her neck, not to say cover it up completely; for it had shrunk and was encircled with wrinkles that had been inaccess-ible to sunburn.

Still seated, she dawdled over tidying away her various odds and ends, and her eyes began to glance round the room, as if some chair were missing. But what she was looking for was her old energy, the old anxiety to see at once that everything was as it should be in her comfortable home.

'Oh! That trip!' she sighed. 'How could I? How exhausting it all is!'

She frowned, once again with that irritable jerk of her chin, when she noticed the broken glass of a little picture by Chaplin which she thought perfectly lovely – the head of a young girl, all silver and rose.

'And I could put both hands through that tear in the lace cur-tains. ... And that's only the beginning. ... What a fool I was to stay away so long! And all in *his* honour! As if I couldn't just as well have nursed my grief here, in peace and comfort!'

She rose, disgruntled, and, gathering up the flounces of her tea-gown, went over to ring the bell, saying to herself, 'Get along with you, you old baggage!'

Her maid entered, under a heap of underclothes and silk stockings.

'Eleven o'clock, Rose. And my face hasn't been done yet. I'm late.'

'There's nothing to be late for. There aren't any old maids now to drag Madame off on excursions, or turn up at crack of dawn to pick every rose in the place. There's no Monsieur Roland to drive Madame mad by throwing pebbles through her window. ...'

'Rose, there's only too much to keep us busy in the house. The proverb may well be true that three moves are as bad as a fire, but I'm quite convinced that being away from home for six months is as bad as a flood. I suppose you've noticed the hole in the curtain?'

'That's nothing. ... Madame has not yet seen the linen-room: mouse-droppings everywhere and holes nibbled in the floor. And it's a funny thing that I left Émérancie with twenty-eight glass-cloths and I come back to find twenty-two.'

'No!'

'It's the truth – every word I say, Madame.'

They looked at each other, sharing the same indignation, both of them deeply attached to this comfortable house, muffled in carpets and silks, with its well-stocked cupboards and its shiny white basement. Léa gave her knee a determined slap.

'We'll soon change all that, my friend. If Ernest and Émérancie don't want their week's notice, they'll manage to find those six glass-cloths. And did you write to Marcel, and tell that great donkey which day to come back?'

'He's here, Madame.'

Léa dressed quickly, then opened the window and leaned out, gazing complacently at her avenue of trees in bud. No more of those fawning old maids, and no more of Monsieur Roland – the athletic young heavyweight at Cambo. ... 'The idiot,' she sighed.

She forgave this passing acquaintance his silliness, and blamed him only for having failed to please her. In her memory – that of a healthy woman with a forgetful body – Monsieur Roland was now only a powerful animal, slightly ridiculous and, when it came to the point, so very clumsy. Léa would now have denied that, one rainy evening when the showers were falling in fragrance on the rose-geraniums, a flood of blinding tears had served to blot out Monsieur Roland behind the image of Chéri.

This brief encounter had left Léa unembarrassed and unregretful. In the villa she had taken at Cambo, the 'idiot' and his frolicking old mother would have been made just as welcome as before. They could have gone on enjoying the well-arranged meals, the rocking-chairs on the wooden balcony, all the creature comforts that Léa dispensed with such justifiable pride. But the idiot had felt sore and gone away, leaving Léa to the attentions of a stiff, handsome officer, greying at the temples, who aspired to marriage with 'Madame de Lonval'.

'Our years, our fortunes, the taste we both have for independence and society, doesn't everything show that we were destined for each other?' murmured the colonel, who still kept his slim waist.

She laughed, and enjoyed the company of this dry, dapper man, who ate well and knew how to hold his liquor. He mistook her feelings and he read into the lovely blue eyes, and the trustful, lingering smiles of his hostess, the acceptance he was expecting. The end of their dawning friendship was marked by a decisive gesture on her part: one she regretted in her heart of hearts and for which she was honest enough to accept the blame. 'It's my own fault. One should never treat a Colonel Ypoustègue, descendant of an ancient Basque family, as one would treat a Monsieur Roland. I've never given any-one such a snub. All the same, it would have been gentlemanly, and intelligent too, if he had come back as usual the next day in his dog-cart, to smoke his cigar, meet the two old girls, and pull their legs.'

She failed to understand that a middle-aged man could accept his dismissal, but not certain glances – glances appraising his physique, comparing him in that respect so unmistakably with another, un-known and invisible. Léa, caught in his sudden kiss, had subjected him to the searching, formidable gaze of a woman who knows exactly where to find the tell-tale marks of age. From the dry, well-cared-for hands, ribbed with veins and tendons, her glance rose to the pouched chin and furrowed brows, returning cruelly to the mouth entrapped between double lines of inverted commas. Where-upon all the aristocratic refinement of the 'Baroness de Lonval' col-lapsed in an 'Oh, la la,' so insulting, so explicit, so common, that the handsome figure of Colonel Ypoustègue passed through her door for the last time.

'The last of my idylls,' Léa was thinking, as she leaned out over her window-ledge. But the weather over Paris was fine, her echoing courtyard was dapper, with its laurel trees rising ball-shaped in green tubs, and from the room behind her a breath of scented warmth came playing over the nape of her neck: all this gradually helped her to recover her good humour, and her sense of mischief. She watched the silhouettes of women passing on their way down to the Bois. 'So skirts are changing again!' Léa observed, 'and hats are higher.' She planned sessions with her dressmaker, others with her milliner; the sudden desire to look beautiful made her straighten her back. 'Beautiful? For whom? Why, for myself, of course. And then to aggravate old Ma Peloux!'

Léa had heard about Chéri's flight, but knew no more than that. While disapproving of Madame Peloux's private-detective methods, she did not scruple to listen to a young *vendeuse*, who would show her gratitude for all Léa's kindnesses by pouring gossip in her ear at a fitting, or else by sending it to her, with 'a thousand thanks for the delicious chocolates' on a huge sheet of paper embossed with the letter-head of her establishment. A postcard from Lili, forwarded to Léa at Cambo – a postcard scribbled by the dotty old harridan in a trembling hand without commas or full stops – had recounted an incomprehensible story of love and flight and a young wife kept under lock and key at Neuilly.

'It was weather like this', Léa recalled, 'the morning I read Lili's postcard in my bath at Cambo.'

She could see the yellow bathroom, the sunlight dancing on the water and ceiling. She could hear the thin-walled villa re-echoing with a great peal of laughter – her own laughter, rather ferocious and none too spontaneous – then the cries that followed it: 'Rose! Rose!'

Breasts and shoulders out of water, dripping, robust, one magnificent arm outstretched, looking more than ever like a naiad on a fountain, she had waved the card with the tips of her wet fingers. 'Rose, Rose! Chéri ... Monsieur Peloux has done a bunk! He's left his wife!'

'That doesn't surprise me, Madame,' Rose had said. 'The divorce will be gayer than the wedding, when the dead seemed to be burying the dead.'

All through that day Léa had given way to unseemly mirth. 'Oh! that fiendish boy. Oh! the naughty child! Just think of it!'

And she shook her head, laughing softly to herself, like a mother whose son has stayed out all night for the first time.

A bright varnished park-phaeton flashed past her gates, sparkled behind its prancing high-steppers and vanished almost without a sound on its rubber wheels.

'There goes Spéleïeff,' Léa observed, 'he's a good sort. And there goes Merguillier on his piebald: eleven o'clock. It won't be long before that dried-up old Berthellemy passes on his way to thaw out his bones on the Sentier de la Vertu. Curious how people can go on doing the same thing day after day! I could almost believe I'd never left Paris, except that Chéri isn't here. My poor Chéri! He's finished with, for the present. Night-life, women, eating at any hour, drinking too much. It's a pity. He might have turned into a decent sort, perhaps, if he'd only had pink chaps like a pork-butcher and flat feet. ...'

She left the window, rubbing her numbed elbows, and shrugged her shoulders. 'Chéri could be saved once, but not a second time.' She polished her nails, breathed on a tarnished ring, peered closely at the disastrous red of her hair and its greying roots, and jotted down a few notes on a pad. She did everything at high speed and with less composure than usual, trying to ward off an attack of her old insidious anxiety. Familiar as this was, she denied its connexion with her grief and called it 'her moral indigestion'. She began wanting first one thing, then suddenly another – a well-sprung victoria with a quiet horse appropriate to a dowager; then a very fast motor-car; then a suite of Directoire furniture. She even thought of doing her hair differently; for twenty years she had worn it high, brushed straight off the neck. 'Rolled curls low on the neck, like Lavallière? Then I should be able to cope with this year's loose-waisted dresses. With a strict diet, in fact, and my hair properly hennaed, I can hope for ten – no, let's say five years more of ...'

With an effort she recovered her good sense, her pride, her lucidity. 'A woman like me would never have the courage to call a halt? Nonsense, my pretty, we've had a good run for our money.' She surveyed the tall figure, erect, hands on hips, smiling at her from the looking-glass. She was still Léa.

'Surely a woman like that doesn't end up in the arms of an old man? A woman like that, who's had the luck never to soil her hands or her mouth on a withered stick! Yes, there she stands, the "vampire", who needs must feed off youthful flesh.'

She conjured up the chance acquaintances and lovers of her early days: always she had escaped elderly lechers; so she felt pure, and proud of thirty years devoted to radiant youths and fragile adolescents.

'And this youthful flesh of theirs certainly owes me a great debt. How many of them have me to thank for their good health, their good looks, the harmlessness of their sorrows! And then their eggnogs when they suffered from colds, and the habit of making love unselfishly and always refreshingly! Shall I now, merely to fill my bed, provide myself with an old gentleman of ... of ...' She hunted about and finished up with majestic forgetfulness of her own age, 'An old gentleman of forty?'

She rubbed her long shapely hands together and turned away in disgust. 'Pooh! Farewell to all that! It's much prettier. Let's go out and buy playing-cards, good wine, bridge-scorers, knitting-needles – all the paraphernalia to fill a gaping void, all that's required to disguise that monster, an old woman.'

In place of knitting-needles she bought a number of dresses, and négligées like the gossamer clouds of dawn. A Chinese pedicure came once a week, the manicurist twice, the masseuse every day. Léa was to be seen at plays, and before the theatre at restaurants where she never thought of going in Chéri's time.

She allowed young women and their friends – as well as Kühn, her former tailor, now retired – to ask her to their box or to their table. But the young women treated her with a deference she did not appreciate; and when Kühn, at their first supper together, called her 'my dear friend', she retorted: 'Kühn, I assure you it doesn't suit you at all to be a customer.'

She sought refuge with Patron, now a referee and boxing promoter. But Patron was married to a young person who ran a bar, a little creature as fierce and jealous as a terrier. To join the susceptible athlete, Léa went as far out as the Place d'Italie, at considerable risk to her dark sapphire-blue dress, heavy with gold embroidery, to her birds of paradise, her impressive jewels, and her new rich red-tinted coiffure. She had had enough after one sniff of the sweat, vinegar, and turpentine exuded by Patron's 'white hopes', and she left, deciding never to venture again inside that long, low, gas-hissing hall.

An unaccountable weariness followed her every attempt to get back into the bustling life of people with nothing to do.

'What can be the matter with me?'

She rubbed her ankles, a little swollen by evening, looked at her strong teeth, and gums that had hardly begun to recede; and thumped her strong ribs and healthy stomach as if sounding a cask. Yet some indefinable weight, now that the chock had been knocked from under her, was shifting within her, and dragging her down. It was the Baroness de la Berche – met by chance in a 'public bar' where she was washing down two dozen snails with cabbies' white wine – who in the end informed her of the prodigal's return to the fold, and of the dawn of a crescent honeymoon in the Boulevard d'Inkermann. Léa listened calmly to this Moral Tale; but she turned pale with emotion the following day when she recognized the blue limousine outside her gates and saw Charlotte Peloux on her way to the house.

'At last, at last! Here you are again, Léa, my beauty! ... Lovelier than ever! Thinner than last year! Take care, Léa, we mustn't get too thin at our age! So far, and no further! And yet ... But what a treat it is to see you!'

Never had that bitter tongue sounded so sweet to Léa. She let Madame Peloux prattle on, thankful for the breathing-space afforded by this acid stream. She had settled Charlotte Peloux into a deep armchair, in the soft light of the little pink-panelled salon, as in the old days. Automatically she had herself taken the straight-backed chair, which forced her to lift her shoulders and keep up her chin, as in the old days. Between them stood the table covered by a cloth of heavy embroidery, and on it, as in the old days, the large cut-glass decanter half full of old brandy, the shimmering petal-thin goblets, iced water, and shortbread biscuits.

'My beauty, now we'll be able to see each other again in peace, in peace. You know my motto: "When in trouble, shun your friends:

let them only share your luck!" All the time Chéri was playing truant, I purposely didn't show you any sign of life, you understand. Now that all's well and my children are happy again, I shout it aloud, I throw myself into your arms, and we start our pleasant existence all over again. ...' She broke off and lit a cigarette, as clever with her pauses as an actress, '... without Chéri, of course.'

'Of course,' Léa acquiesced with a smile.

She was watching and listening to her old enemy in satisfied astonishment. The huge inhuman eyes, the chattering lips, the restless, tight little body – all that was facing her across the table had come simply to test her powers of resistance, to humiliate her, as in the old days, always as in the old days. But, as in the old days, Léa knew when to answer, when to be scornful, when to smile, and when to retaliate. Already that sorry burden, which had weighed so heavily the day before and the days before that, was beginning slowly to lift. The light seemed normal once more, and familiar, as it played over the curtains and suffused the little drawing-room.

'Here we are again,' Léa thought, in lighter vein. 'Two women, both a little older than a year ago, the same habits of backbiting and the same stock phrases; good-natured wariness at meals shared together; the financial papers in the morning, scandalmongering in the afternoon: all this will have to be taken up again, since it's Life, my life. The Aldonzas and the de la Berches, the Lilis, and a few homeless old gentlemen: the whole lot squeezed round a card table, with the packs jostling the brandy-glasses, and perhaps, thrown in, a pair of little woollen shoes, begun for a baby who's soon to be born. ... We'll start all over again, since it is ordained. Let's enter on it cheerfully. After all, it's only too easy to sink back into the grooves of the old life.'

And she settled back, eyes bright and mouth relaxed, to listen to Charlotte Peloux, who was greedily expatiating upon her daughter-in-law.

'My Léa, you should know, if anyone, that what I've always longed for is peace and quiet. Well now, I've got them. Chéri's escapade, you see, was nothing more than sowing a few wild oats. Far be it from me to reproach you, Léa dear, but as you'll be the first to admit, from eighteen to twenty-five he really never had the time to lead the life of a bachelor! And now he's done it with a vengeance!'

'It's a very good thing that he did,' Léa said, without the flicker of a smile; 'it acts as a sort of guarantee to his wife for the future.'

'The very word, the very word I was hunting for!' barked Madame Peloux, beaming. 'A guarantee! And ever since that day – one long dream! And, you know, when a Peloux does come home again after being properly out on the spree, he never goes off again!'

'Is that a family tradition?' Léa asked.

But Charlotte took no notice.

'And what's more, he was very well received when he did return home. His little wife – ah, there's a little wife for you, Léa! – and I've seen a fair number of little wives in my time, you know, and I don't mind telling you I've never seen one to hold a candle to Edmée!'

'Her mother is so remarkable,' Léa said.

'Think, just think, my beauty – Chéri left her on my hands for very nearly three months! and between you and me she was very lucky to have me there.'

'That's exactly what I was thinking,' Léa said.

'And then, my dear, never a word of complaint, never a scene, never a tactless word! Nothing, nothing! She was patience itself, and sweetness … and the face of a saint, a saint!'

'It's terrifying,' Léa said.

'And then, what d'you suppose happened when our young rascal walked in one morning, all smiles, as though he'd just come in from a stroll in the Bois? D'you suppose she allowed herself a single comment? Not one. Far from it. Nothing. As for him, though at heart he must have felt just a little ashamed …'

'Oh, why?' Léa asked.

'Well, really! After all … He was welcomed with open arms, and the whole thing was put right in their bedroom – in two ticks – just like that – no time lost! Oh, I can assure you, for the next hour or so there wasn't a happier woman in the world than me.'

'Except, perhaps, Edmée,' Léa suggested.

But Madame Peloux was all exaltation, and executed a superb soaring movement with her little arms: 'I don't know what you can be thinking of. Personally, I was only thinking of the happy hearth and home.'

She changed her tune, screwed up her eyes, and pouted: 'Besides, I can't see that little girl frantic with passion, or sobbing with ecstasy. Twenty, and skinny at that. ... Pah! at that age they stammer and stutter. And then, between ourselves, I think her mother's cold.'

'Aren't you being carried away by your sense of family?' Léa said.

Charlotte Peloux expanded her eyes to show their very depths, but absolutely nothing was to be read there.

'Certainly not, certainly not! Heredity, heredity! I'm a firm believer in it. Look at my son, who is fantasy incarnate ... What? You don't know that he's fantasy incarnate?'

'It must have escaped my memory,' Léa apologized.

'Well, I have high hopes for my son's future. He'll love his home as I love mine, he'll look after his fortune, he'll love his children, as I loved him. ...'

'For goodness' sake, don't paint such a depressing picture,' Léa begged. 'What's it like, the young people's home?'

'Sinister!' shrieked Madame Peloux. 'Positively sinister. Purple carpets. Purple! A black-and-gold bathroom. A salon with no furniture in it, full of Chinese vases larger than me! So, what happens is that they're always at Neuilly. Besides, without being conceited, I must say that girl adores me.'

'Her nerves have not been upset at all?' Léa asked anxiously.

Charlotte Peloux's eyes brightened. 'No danger of that! She plays her hand well, and we must face the fact.'

'Who d'you mean by "we"?'

'Forgive me, my beauty, pure habit. We're dealing here with what I call a brain, a real brain. You should see the way she gives orders without raising her voice, and takes Chéri's teasing, and swallows the bitterest pills as if they were lollipops. ... I begin to wonder, I really begin to wonder, whether there is not positive danger lying ahead for my son. I'm afraid, Léa dear, I'm afraid she may prove a damper on his originality, on –'

'What? Is he being an obedient little boy?' Léa interrupted. 'Do have some more of my brandy, Charlotte, it comes from Spéleïeff and it's seventy-four years old – you could give it to a new-born babe.'

' "Obedient" is hardly the right word, but he's ... inter – impertur –'

92

'Imperturbable?'

'That's the word! For instance, when he knew I was coming to see you ...'

'Did he know, then?'

An impetuous blush leapt to Léa's cheeks, and she cursed her hot blood and the bright daylight of the little drawing-room. Madame Peloux, a benign expression in her eyes, fed on Léa's confusion.

'But of course he knew. That oughtn't to bring a blush to your cheeks, my beauty. What a child you are!'

'In the first place, how did you know I was back?'

'Oh, come, Léa, don't ask such foolish questions. You've been seen about everywhere.'

'Yes, but Chéri – did you tell him I was back?'

'No, my beauty, it was he who told me.'

'Oh, it was he who ... That's funny.'

She heard her heart beating in her voice and dared not risk more than the shortest answers.

'He even added: "Madame Peloux, you'll oblige me by going to find out news of Nounoune." He's still so fond of you, the dear boy.'

'How nice!'

Madame Peloux, crimson in the face, seemed to abandon herself to the influence of the old brandy and talked as in a dream, wagging her head from side to side. But her russet eyes remained fixed and steely, and she kept a close watch on Léa, who was sitting bolt upright, armed against herself, waiting for the next thrust.

'It's nice, but it's quite natural. A man doesn't forget a woman like you, Léa dear. And ... if you want to know what I really think, you've only to lift a finger and ...'

Léa put a hand on Charlotte Peloux's arm. 'I don't want to know what you really think,' she said gently.

The corners of Madame Peloux's mouth fell: 'Oh, I can understand, I approve,' she sighed in a passionless voice. 'When one has made other arrangements for one's life, as you have ... I haven't even had a word with you about yourself!'

'But it seems to me that you have.'

'Happy?'

'Happy.'

'Divinely happy? A lovely trip? Is *he* nice? Where's his photo?'

Léa, relieved, sharpened her smile and shook her head. 'No, no, you'll find out nothing, search where you will. Have your detectives let you down, Charlotte?'

'I rely on no detectives,' Charlotte answered. 'It's certainly not because anyone has told me ... that you'd been through another heart-breaking desertion ... that you'd been terribly worried, even over money. ... No, no, you know what small attention I pay to gossip!'

'No one knows it better than me. My dear Lolotte, you can go back home without any fears on my behalf. And please reassure our friends, and tell them that I only wish they had made half what I did out of Oil shares between December and February.'

The alcoholic cloud-screen, which softened the features of Madame Peloux, lifted in a trice; a clear, sharp, thoroughly alert face emerged. 'You were in on Oil? I might have known it! And you never breathed a word to me.'

'You never asked me about it. ... You were thinking only of your family, as was natural. ...'

'Fortunately, I was thinking of Compressed Fuel at the same time.' The muted trumpet resembled a flute.

'Ah! and you never let on to me either!'

'Intrude upon love's young dream? Never! Léa, my dear, I'm off now, but I'll be back.'

'You'll come back on Thursday, because at present, my dear Lolotte, your Sundays at Neuilly ... they're finished for me. Would you like it if I started having a few people here on Thursdays? Nobody except old friends, old Ma Aldonza, our Reverend-Father-the-Baronet – poker for you, knitting for me. ...'

'Do you knit?'

'Not yet, but it will soon come. Well?'

'I jump for joy at the idea! See if I'm not jumping! And you may be sure I won't say a word about it at home. That bad boy would be quite capable of coming and asking for a glass of port on one of your Thursdays. Just one more little kiss, my beauty. ... Heavens, how good you smell. Have you noticed that as the skin gets less firm, the scent sinks in better and lasts much longer? It's really very nice.'

'Be off, be off. ...' Quivering, Léa stood watching Madame Peloux as she crossed the courtyard. 'Go on your mischievous way! Nothing can stop you. You twist your ankle, yes – but it never brings you down. Your chauffeur is careful not to skid, so you'll never crash into a tree. You'll get back safely to Neuilly, and you'll choose your moment – today, or tomorrow, or one day next week – to come out with words that should never pass your lips. You'll try and upset those who, perhaps, are happy and at peace. The least harm you'll do is to make them tremble a little, as you made me, for a moment. ...'

She was trembling at the knees, like a horse after a steep pull, but she was not in pain. She felt overjoyed at having kept so strict a control over herself and her words. Her looks and her colour were enhanced by her recent encounter, and she went on pulping her handkerchief to release her bottled-up energy.

She could not detach her thoughts from Madame Peloux. 'We've come together again,' she said to herself, 'like two dogs over an old slipper which both have got used to chewing. How queer it is! That woman is my enemy, and yet it's from her I now draw my comfort. How close are the ties that bind us!'

Thus, for a long time, she mused over her future, veering between alarm and resignation. Her nerves were relaxed, and she slept for a little. As she sat with one cheek pressed against a cushion, her dreams projected her into her fast-approaching old age. She saw day follow day with clockwork monotony, and herself beside Charlotte Peloux – their spirited rivalry helping the time to pass. In this way she would be spared, for many years, the degrading listlessness of women past their prime, who abandon first their stays, then their hair-dye, and who finally no longer bother about the quality of their underclothes. She had a foretaste of the sinful pleasures of the old – little else than a concealed aggressiveness, day-dreams of murder, and the keen recurrent hope for catastrophes that will spare only one living creature and one corner of the globe. Then she woke up, amazed to find herself in the glow of a pink twilight as roseate as the dawn.

'Ah, Chéri!' she sighed.

But it was no longer the raucous hungry cry of a year ago. She was not now in tears, nor was her body suffering and rebellious, because threatened by some sickness of the soul. Léa rose from her chair, and rubbed her cheek, embossed by the imprint of the embroidered cushion.

'My poor Chéri! It's a strange thought that the two of us – you by losing your worn old mistress, and I by losing my scandalous young lover – have each been deprived of the most honourable possession we had upon this earth!'

Two days went by after the visit of Charlotte Peloux: two grey days that passed slowly for Léa. She faced this new life with the patience of an apprentice. 'Since this is going to be my new life,' she said to herself, 'I'd better make a start.' But she set about it clumsily, altogether too conscientiously, so that it was a strain on her perseverance. On the second day, about eleven in the morning, she was seized with a desire to go for a walk through the Bois as far as the Lakes.

'I'll buy a dog,' she thought. 'He'll be a companion, and force me to walk.' And Rose had to hunt through the bottom of the summer cupboards for a pair of strong-soled brown boots and a tweed coat and skirt, smelling of alpine meadows and pine forests. Léa set off with the resolute stride proper to the wearer of heavy footwear and rough country clothes.

'Ten years ago, I should not have feared to carry a stick,' she said to herself. When still quite near the house, she heard behind her a brisk light tread, which she thought she recognized. She became unnerved, almost paralysed by a compelling fear; and before she could recover she let herself unwittingly be overtaken, and then passed, by an unknown young man. He was in a hurry, and never even glanced at her.

'I really am a fool,' she breathed in her relief.

She bought a dark carnation to pin on her jacket and started off again. But thirty yards ahead of her, looming out of the diaphanous mist above the grass verges of the Avenue, the silhouette of a man was waiting.

'This time I do recognize the cut of that coat and that way of twirling a cane. ... Oh, no thank you, the last thing I want is for him to see me shod like a postman and wearing a thick jacket that makes me look stocky. If I must run into him, I'd far rather he saw me in something else ... and he never could stand me in brown, anyhow. ... No, no ... I'm off home. ... I ...'

At that moment the waiting man hailed an empty taxi, stepped in, and drove past Léa: he was a young man with fair hair and a small close-clipped moustache. But this time Léa did not smile or feel relief. She turned on her heel and walked back home.

'One of my off-days, Rose. ... Bring me the peach-blossom tea-gown, the new one, and the big embroidered cloak. I'm stifling in these woollen things.'

'It's no good being obstinate,' Léa thought. 'Twice in succession it's turned out not to be Chéri: the third time it would have been. I know the little jokes Fate plays on one. There's nothing to be done about it. I've no fight left in me today, I'm feeling limp.'

She spent the rest of the day once more trying patiently to learn to be alone. After luncheon she enjoyed a cigarette and a look at the papers, and welcomed with a short-lived joy a telephone call from Baroness de la Berche, then another from Spéleïeff, her former lover, the handsome horse-coper, who had seen her in the street the previous evening and offered to sell her a spanking pair.

There followed an hour of complete and frightening silence. 'Come, come ...' She began to walk up and down, with her hands on her hips, her arms free of the heavy gold rose-embroidered cloak, its magnificent train sweeping the floor behind her.

'Come, come. ... Let's try to take stock. This isn't the moment to become demoralized – now that I'm no longer in love with the boy. I've been living on my own now for six months. I managed perfectly well when I was in the south. To start with, I moved about from place to place. And the people I got to know on the Riviera or in the Pyrenees did me good; I felt positively refreshed each time any of them went away. Starch poultices may not cure a burn, but they do bring relief when constantly renewed. My six months of keeping on the move reminds me of the story of that hideous Sarah Cohen, who married a monster of ugliness. "Each time I look at him, I think that I am pretty."

'But I knew what it was like to live alone before these last six months. What sort of life did I lead after I'd left Spéleïeff, for instance? Oh yes, I went chasing round bistros and bars with Patron, and then all of a sudden Chéri came into my life. But before Spéleïeff, there was little Lequellec: when his family dragged him away from me to lead him to the altar, his beautiful eyes were brimming with tears, poor boy. ... After him, I was all alone for four months, I remember. The first month, I cried a great deal. Oh, no, it was for Bacciocchi I cried so much. But when I was through with my tears, there was no holding me. It was so delightful to find myself alone. Yes, but at the Bacciocchi time I was twenty-eight, and thirty after Lequellec, and in between these two, I had known ... Well, no matter. After Spéleïeff, I became disgusted – so much money so ill spent. Whereas now, after Chéri, I'm ... I'm fifty, and I was unwise enough to keep him for six whole years!'

She wrinkled her forehead, and looked ugly with her mouth in a sulky droop.

'It serves me right. At my age, one can't afford to keep a lover six years. Six years! He has ruined all that was left of me. Those six years might have given me two or three quite pleasant little happinesses, instead of one profound regret. A liaison of six years is like following your husband out to the colonies: when you get back again nobody recognizes you and you've forgotten how to dress.'

To relieve the strain, she rang for Rose, and together they went through the contents of the little cupboard where she kept her lace. Night fell, set the lamps blossoming into light, and called Rose back to the cares of the house.

'Tomorrow,' Léa said to herself, 'I'll order the motor and drive out to Spéleïeff's stud-farm in Normandy. I'll take old La Berche, if she wants to come: it will remind her of the past glories of her own carriages. And, upon my word, should the younger Spéleïeff cast an eye in my direction, I'm not saying I ...'

She carefully smiled a mysterious and provocative smile, to delude what ghosts there might be hovering round the dressing-table or round the formidable bed, glimmering in the shadows. But she felt entirely frigid, and full of contempt for the pleasures other people found in love.

She dined off grilled sole and pastries, and found the meal a recreation. She chose a dry champagne in place of the Bordeaux, and hummed as she left the table. Eleven o'clock caught her by surprise, still taking the measurements of the space between the windows in her bedroom, where she planned to replace the large looking-glasses with old painted panels of flowers and balustrades. She yawned, scratched her head, and rang for her maid to undress her. While Rose knelt to take off her silk stockings, Léa reviewed her achievements of the day already slipping into the pages of the past, and was as pleased with her performance as if she had polished off an imposition. Protected for the night against the dangers of idleness, she could look forward to so many hours of sleep, so many when she would lie awake. Under cover of night, the restless regain the privilege of yawning aloud or sighing, of cursing the milkman's cart, the street-cleaners, and the early morning sparrows.

During her preparations for the night, she thought over a number of mild projects that would never come into being.

'Aline Mesmacker has a restaurant bar and is simply coining money. ... Obviously, it gives her something to do, as well as being a good investment. ... But I can't see myself sitting at a cash-desk; and if one employs a manageress, it's no longer worth while. Dora and that fat Fifi run a night club together, Mother La Berche told me. Everybody's doing it now. And they wear stiff collars and dinner jackets, to attract a special clientèle. Fat Fifi has three children to bring up – they're her excuse. ... Then there's Kühn, who's simply kicking his heels, and would gladly take some of my capital to start a new dressmaker's.' Naked, and brick-pink from the reflection of her Pompeian bathroom, she sprayed herself with her favourite sandalwood, and, without thinking about it, enjoyed unfolding a long silk nightgown.

'All that's so much poppycock! I know perfectly well that I dislike working. To bed with you, Madame! You'll never have any other place of business, and all your customers are gone!'

The coloured lining of the white gandoura she put on was suffused with a vague pink. She went back to her dressing-table, and combed and tugged at the hairs stiffened by dye, lifting both her arms, and thus framing her tired face. Her arms were still so beautiful, from the full deep hollow of the armpit up to the rounded wrists, that she sat gazing at them in the looking-glass.

'What lovely handles for so old a vase!'

With a careless gesture she thrust a pale tortoiseshell comb into the back of her hair, and, without much hope, picked a detective story from the shelf of a dark closet. She had no taste for fine bindings and had never lost the habit of relegating books to the bottom of a cupboard, along with cardboard boxes and empty medicine bottles.

As she stood smoothing the cool linen sheets on her huge uncovered bed, the big bell in the courtyard rang out. The full, solemn, unwonted peal jarred on the midnight hour.

'What in the world ...?' she said out loud.

She held her breath while listening, her lips parted. A second peal sounded even louder than the first, and Léa, with an instinctive movement of self-preservation and modesty, ran to powder her face. She was about to ring for Rose when she heard the front door slam, followed by footsteps in the hall and on the stairs, and the sound of two voices mingling – her maid's and someone else's. She had no time to make up her mind: the door of her room was flung open by a ruthless hand. Chéri stood before her – his top-coat unbuttoned over evening clothes, his hat on his head – pale and angry-looking.

He leaned back against the door now shut behind him, and did not move. He looked not so much at Léa as all round the room, with the quick shifting glance of a man about to be attacked.

Léa, who that morning had trembled at the half-surmised outline of a figure in the mist, felt at first only the resentment of a woman caught at her toilet. She drew her wrap more closely about her, settled her comb, and with one foot hunted for a missing slipper. She blushed, yet by the time the high colour died down she had already recovered the semblance of calm. She raised her head and appeared taller than the young man who was leaning, all in black, against the white of the door.

'That's a nice way to come into a room,' she said in a rather loud voice. 'You might at least take your hat off and say good evening.'

'Good evening,' Chéri said in surly tones.

The sound of his voice seemed to astonish him. He looked all about less like an angry animal, and a sort of smile drifted from his eyes down to his mouth, as he repeated a gentler 'Good evening'.

He took off his hat and came forward a few steps.

'May I sit down?'

'If you like,' Léa said.

He sat down on a pouffe and saw that she remained standing.

'Are you in the middle of dressing? Aren't you going out?'

She shook her head, sat down far away from him, picked up her nail-buffer, and never said a word. He lit a cigarette, and asked her permission only after it was alight.

'If you like,' Léa repeated indifferently.

He said nothing more and dropped his gaze. Noticing that his hand with the cigarette in it was shaking, he rested it on the edge of a table. Léa continued polishing her nails deliberately and from time to time cast a brief glance at Chéri's face, especially at his lowered eyelids and the dark fringe of his lashes.

'It was Ernest who opened the front door to me as usual,' Chéri said at last.

'And why shouldn't it have been Ernest? Ought I to have changed my staff because you got married?'

'No ... I mean, I simply said that ...'

Again silence fell, broken by Léa.

'May I know whether you intend to remain for some time, sitting on that pouffe? I don't even ask why you take the liberty of entering my house at midnight. ...'

'You may ask me why,' he said quickly.

She shook her head. 'It doesn't interest me.'

He jumped up precipitously, sending the pouffe rolling away behind him, and bore down upon Léa. She felt him bending over her as if he were going to strike her, but she did not flinch. The thought came to her: 'What in this world is there for me to be frightened of?'

'So you don't know what brings me here! You don't want to know what brings me here!'

He tore off his coat and sent it flying on to the chaise-longue, then he crossed his arms, and shouted quite close to Léa's face, in a strained but triumphant voice, 'I've come back!'

She was using a delicate pair of tweezers, and these she carefully put away before wiping her fingers. Chéri dropped into a chair, as though his strength was completely exhausted.

'Good,' Léa said. 'You've come back. That's very nice! Whose advice did you take about that?'

'My own,' Chéri said.

She got up in her turn, the better to dominate him. Her surging heartbeats had subsided, allowing her to breathe in comfort. She wanted to play her role without a mistake.

'Why didn't you ask me for my advice? I'm an old friend who knows all your clownish ways. Why did it never occur to you that your coming here might well embarrass ... someone?'

Lowering his head, he searched every corner of the room from under his eyebrows – the closed doors, the bed, metal-girt and heaped with luxurious pillows. He found nothing exceptional, nothing new, and shrugged his shoulders.

Léa expected more than that and drove home her point. 'You understand what I mean?'

'Perfectly,' he answered. ' "Monsieur" has not come in yet? "Monsieur" is sleeping out?'

'That's none of your business, child,' she said calmly.

He bit his lip and nervously knocked off his cigarette ash into a jewel tray.

'Not in that, I keep on telling you!' Léa cried. 'How many times must I ...?'

She broke off to reproach herself for having unconsciously adopted the tone of their old familiar quarrels. But he did not appear to have heard and went on examining one of Léa's rings – an emerald she had purchased on her recent trip.

'What's ... what's this?' he stammered.

'That? It's an emerald.'

'I'm not blind. What I mean is, who gave it you?'

'No one you know.'

'Charming!' Chéri said bitterly.

The note in his voice was enough to restore Léa's authority, and she pressed her advantage, taking pleasure in leading him still further astray.

'Isn't it charming! I get compliments on it wherever I go. And the setting you've seen it ... the filigree of diamonds ...'

'Enough!' bawled Chéri furiously, smashing his fist down on the fragile table.

A few roses shed their petals at the impact, and a china cup slithered without breaking on to the thick carpet. Léa reached for the telephone, but Chéri caught her hand in a rough grasp. 'What are you going to do with that telephone?'

'Call the police,' Léa said.

He took hold of both her arms, pretending to be up to some playful nonsense as he pushed her away from the instrument.

'Oh, go on with you, that's all right. Don't be silly! Can't I even open my mouth without your getting all melodramatic?'

She sat down and turned her back on him. He remained standing, with nothing in his hands: his parted lips were swollen, giving him the look of a sulky child; one black lock hung down over his eyebrow. Surreptitiously, Léa watched him in a looking-glass, till his reflection vanished when he sat down. In her turn, Léa was embarrassed when she felt him staring at her back, broadened by the loose folds of her gandoura. She returned to her dressing-table, smoothed her hair, rearranged her comb, and, as if for want of something better to do, began unscrewing the top of a scent-bottle. Chéri turned his head as the first whiff reached his nostrils.

'Nounoune!' he called.

She did not answer.

'Nounoune!'

'Beg my pardon,' she ordered, without turning round.

'Not likely!' he sneered.

'I can't force you. But you'll leave the house. And at once. ...'

'I beg your pardon,' he said at once peevishly.

'Better than that.'

'I beg your pardon,' he repeated, quite low.

'That's better.'

She went over to him and ran her hand lightly over his bowed head. 'Come, tell me all about it.'

He shivered, trembling under her touch. 'What do you want me to tell you? It's not very complicated. I've come back, that's all.'

'Tell me! Come along, tell me!'

He rocked backwards and forwards on his seat, pressing his hands between his knees, and raised his head towards Léa without meeting her eyes. She watched the quivering of his nostrils, and she heard him trying to control his rapid breathing. She had only to say once more, 'Come, tell me all about it,' and give him a prod with her finger, as if to push him over. At once he cried out, 'Nounoune darling! Nounoune darling!' and threw all his weight upon her, clasping her long legs, so that they gave way under her.

Once seated, she let him slither to the floor and sprawl over her with tears, and inarticulate words, and groping fingers that caught at her lace and her pearls and hunted feverishly under her dress for the shape of her shoulder and under her hair to touch her ears.

'Nounoune darling! We're together again, my Nounoune! Oh, my Nounoune! your shoulder, and your scent, and your pearls, my Nounoune, oh, it's so stunning ... and that little burnt taste your hair has, oh, it's ... it's stunning. ...'

He leaned back to breathe out this silly word with what might have been the last breath of his body: then, still on his knees, he clasped Léa in his arms, offering her a forehead shadowed under tousled hair, a trembling mouth moist with tears, and eyes bright with weeping and happiness. She was so lost in contemplating him, so perfectly oblivious of everything that was not Chéri, that she never thought of kissing him. She twined her arms round his neck and gently hugged him to her, rocking him to the rhythm of murmured words.

'My pet ... my naughty boy ... You're here ... You've come back again. ... What have you been up to now? You're so naughty ... my pretty. ...'

He was moaning softly, keeping his lips together and hardly speaking, as he listened to Léa. He rested his cheek on her breast and begged her to go on, if for a moment she ceased her tender lullaby. And Léa, fearful that her own tears would flow, went on with her scolding.

'Wicked monster ... heartless little devil ... Get along with you, you great slut!'

He looked at her in gratitude: 'That's right ... Go on slanging me! Oh, Nounoune!'

She held him at arm's length to see him properly. 'So you love me, then?'

He lowered his eyes in childish confusion: 'Yes, Nounoune.'

A little burst of uncontrollable laughter warned Léa that she was on the verge of giving way to the most terrible joy of her life. An embrace, followed by collapse, the uncovered bed, two bodies joined together like the two living halves of an animal that has been cut through. 'No, no,' she said to herself, 'not yet, oh, not yet. ...'

'I'm thirsty,' Chéri sighed. 'Nounoune, I'm thirsty'

She rose quickly and put a hand on the now tepid jug of water; hardly had she hurried from the room before she was back again. Chéri, curled up in a ball, was lying with his head on the pouffe. 'Rose will bring you some lemonade,' Léa said. 'Don't stay there. Come and sit on the chaise-longue. Does the lamp hurt your eyes?'

She was trembling with delight in her imperious solicitude. She sat down at the other end of the chaise-longue and Chéri half stretched out to nestle against her.

'Perhaps now you'll tell me a little ...'

They were interrupted by the entry of Rose. Chéri, without getting up, languidly turned his head in her direction: 'Evening, Rose.'

'Good evening, Monsieur,' Rose said discreetly.

'Rose, tomorrow at nine, I'd like –'

'Brioches and chocolate,' Rose finished for him.

Chéri shut his eyes again with a sigh of contentment. 'And that's that. ... Rose, where am I going to dress tomorrow morning?'

'In the boudoir,' Rose answered accommodatingly. 'Only I had better take the settee out, I suppose, and put back the shaving-mirror, as it used to be?'

She sought confirmation in the eye of Léa, who was proudly displaying her spoilt child, supported by her arm as he drank.

'If you like,' Léa said. 'We'll see. You can go, Rose.'

Rose retired, and during the ensuing moment's silence nothing could be heard except the vague murmuring of the wind and the cry of a bird bewildered by the brightness of the moon.

'Chéri, are you asleep?'

He gave one of his long-drawn sighs like an exhausted retriever. 'Oh, no, Nounoune, I'm too happy to sleep.'

'Tell me, child ... You haven't been unkind over there?'

'At home? No, Nounoune, far from it. I swear to you.'

He looked up at her, without raising his trusting head.

'Of course not, Nounoune. I left because I left. The girl's very nice. There was no fuss at all.'

'Ah!'

'I wouldn't swear that she didn't have an inkling all the same. This evening she was wearing what I call her "orphanage look", you know, pathetic dark eyes under her pretty head of hair. ... You know how pretty her hair is?'

'Yes.'

She threw out these monosyllables in a whisper as if intent on the words of someone talking in his sleep.

'I even think', Chéri continued, 'that she must have seen me going through the garden.'

'Oh?'

'Yes. She was on the balcony, in her white sequin dress, congealed whiteness. Oh! I don't like that dress. ... Ever since dinner it had been making me long to cut and run.'

'No.'

'Yes it had, Nounoune. I can't say whether she saw me. The moon wasn't up. It came up while I was waiting.'

'Where were you waiting?'

Chéri waved a vague hand in the direction of the avenue. 'There. I was waiting, don't you understand. I wanted to see. I'd waited a long time.'

'But what for?'

He hastily jumped away and sat further off. He resumed his expression of primitive distrust. 'I wanted to be sure there was nobody here.'

'Oh, yes. ... You thought that ...'

She could not resist a scornful laugh. A lover in her house! A lover while Chéri was still living! It was grotesque. 'How stupid he is!' she thought in her enthusiasm.

'You're laughing?'

He stood up in front of her and put his hand on her forehead, forcing back her head. 'You're laughing! You're making fun of me. You're ... Then you have a lover! There is someone!'

He leaned over her as he spoke, pushing her head back against the end of the chaise-longue. She felt the breath of an insulting mouth on her eyelids, and made no effort to be free of the hand that was crushing her hair against her forehead.

'I dare you to say you have a lover!'

She fluttered her eyelids, dazzled by the radiance of the face bearing down on her, and finally, in a toneless voice, she said: 'No, I have no lover. I ... love you. ...'

He relaxed his hold and began pulling off his dinner jacket and waistcoat; his tie whistled through the air and ended up round the neck of Léa's bust – up on the mantelpiece. Meanwhile, he never moved away from her, and kept her, wedged between his knees, where she sat on the chaise-longue.

When she saw him half-naked, she asked, with a note of sadness: 'Do you really want to? ... Do you? ...'

He did not answer, carried away by the thought of his approaching pleasure and the consuming desire to take her again. She gave way and served her young lover like a good mistress, with devout solicitude. Nevertheless, she anticipated with a sort of terror the moment of her own undoing; she endured Chéri as she might a torture, warding him off with strengthless hands, and holding him fast between strong knees. Finally, she seized him by the arm, uttered a feeble cry, and foundered in the deep abyss, whence love emerges pale and in silence, regretful of death.

They remained enfolded in their close embrace and no words troubled the prolonged silence of their return to life. The upper part of his body had slipped down and he lay across Léa's thigh, his pendent head, with eyes closed, resting upon the sheets as if he had been stabbed to death over the body of his mistress. She, meanwhile, partly turned away from him, bore almost the full weight of this unsparing body. She breathed softly but unevenly. Her left arm ached, crushed beneath her. Chéri could feel the back of his neck growing numb. Both were waiting, concentrated and motionless, for the abating tempest of their pleasure to recede.

'He's asleep,' Léa thought. With her free hand, she was still clinging to Chéri's wrist, and she squeezed it gently. One of her knees was being crushed by a knee – how well she knew its lovely shape! About the level of her own heart she could feel the steady muffled beating of another. Chéri's favourite scent – insistent, clinging, reminding her of fat waxy flowers and exotic glades – was all pervasive. 'He is here!' she whispered, immersed in a feeling of blind security. 'He is here for ever!' her senses re-echoed. The well-ordered prudence, the happy common sense that had been her guide through life, the humiliating vagaries of her riper years and the subsequent renunciations, all beat a retreat and vanished into thin air before the presumptuous brutality of love. 'He is here!' she thought. 'He has left his own home and his pretty silly little wife to come back, to come back to me! Who can take him from me now? Now at last I'll be able to organize our existence. He doesn't always know what he wants; but I do. No doubt we shall have to go away. We shan't go into hiding, but we'll look for somewhere peaceful. For I must find time to look at him. When I was unaware I loved him, I can't ever have looked at him properly. I must find a place where there'll be room enough for his whims and my wishes. I'll do the thinking for both of us – let him do the sleeping.'

While she was painstakingly withdrawing her left arm, cramped and pricking with pins and needles, and her numbed shoulder, she glanced at Chéri's averted face and found that he was not asleep. She could see the whites of his eyes and the flutter of the little black wings of his long eyelashes.

'Why, you're not asleep!'

She felt him tremble against her, before he turned over in a single movement.

'But you're not asleep, either, Nounoune!'

He stretched a hand out to the bedside table and switched on the lamp: a flood of rosy light covered the big bed, throwing the patterns of the lace into high relief, hollowing out shadowed valleys between swelling hills in the quilted folds of the eiderdown. Chéri, stretched out at full length, surveyed the field of his victory and of his peace. Léa, leaning on one elbow beside him, stroked his beloved, long eyebrows, and swept back the rebellious locks. Lying with his hair dishevelled over his forehead, he looked as if he had been blown over by a raging wind.

The enamel clock struck. Chéri straightened himself at a bound and sat up. 'What time is it?'

'I don't know. What difference can it make to us?'

'Oh, I just asked. ...'

He gave a short laugh, and did not immediately lie down again. Outside, the first milkcart clinked out its tinkling carillon, and he made a vague movement in the direction of the avenue. The strawberry-coloured curtains were slit through by the cold blade of dawning day. Chéri turned back to look at Léa, and stared at her with the formidable intensity of a suspicious dog or a puzzled child. An undecipherable thought appeared in the depths of his eyes; their shape, their dark wallflower hue, their harsh or languorous glint, were used only to win love, never to reveal his mind. From sheets crumpled as though by a storm, rose his naked body, broad-shouldered, slim-waisted; and his whole being breathed forth the melancholy of perfect works of art.

'Ah, you ...' sighed the infatuated Léa.

He did not smile, accustomed as he was to accepting personal praise.

'Tell me, Nounoune. ...'

'What, my pretty?'

He hesitated, fluttered his eyelids, and shivered. 'I'm tired ... and then tomorrow, how will you manage about –'

Léa gave him a gentle push and pulled the naked body and drowsy head down to the pillows again.

'Don't worry. Lie down and go to sleep. Isn't Nounoune here to look after you? Don't think of anything. Sleep. You're cold, I'm sure. ... Here, take this, it's warm. ...'

She rolled him up in the silk and wool of a little feminine garment, retrieved from somewhere in the bed, and put out the light. In the dark, she lent him her shoulder, settled him happily against her side, and listened till his breathing was in rhythm with her own. No desires clouded her mind, but she did not wish for sleep. 'Let him do the sleeping; it's for me to do the thinking,' she repeated to herself. 'I'll contrive our flight with perfect tact and discretion; I believe in causing as little suffering and scandal as possible. ... For the spring we shall like the south best. If there were only myself to be considered, I'd rather stay here, in peace and quiet; but there's Ma Peloux and the young Madame Peloux. ...' The vision of a young wife in her nightgown, anxiously standing beside a window, checked Léa only long enough for her to shrug her shoulders with cold impartiality. 'I can't help that. What makes one person's happiness ...'

The black silky head stirred on her breast, and her sleeping lover moaned in his dream. With a zealous arm, Léa shielded him against nightmares, and rocked him gently so that – without sight, without memory, without plans for the future – he might still resemble that 'naughty little boy' never born to her.

HE had lain awake for some little while, taking great care not to stir. Cheek on folded arms, he tried to guess the time. Under a clear sky, the avenue must be vibrating with heat too insistent for early morning, since no shadow of a cloud passed across the lambent rose-red curtains. 'Ten o'clock, perhaps?' He was tormented by hunger; he had eaten little the previous evening. A year ago he would have bounded out of bed, roughly aroused Léa from sleep by ferocious shouts for cream-frothed chocolate and butter off the ice.

He did not stir. He was afraid, did he move, of crumbling away what remained to him of his rapture, the visual pleasure he derived from the shining curtains and from the steel and brass spirals of the bed, twinkling in the coloured aura of the room. Last night's great happiness had dwindled, it seemed, had melted, and sought refuge in the dancing iridescence of a cut-glass jug.

On the landing, Rose trod the carpet with circumspect step; a discreet besom was sweeping the courtyard; and Chéri heard the tinkle of china coming from the pantry. 'How the morning drags on,' he said to himself. 'I'll get up.' But he remained without moving a muscle, for, behind him, Léa yawned and stretched her legs. He felt the touch of a gentle hand on his back. He shut his eyes again, and, for no good reason, his whole body began to act a lie, feigning the limpness of sleep. He was aware of Léa leaving the bed and of her dark silhouette between him and the curtains, which she drew half apart. She turned round to look at him, and with a toss of the head smiled in his direction – in no sense a smile of triumph, but a resolute smile, ready to accept all dangers. She was in no hurry to leave the room, and Chéri kept watch on her through hardly parted eyelashes. He saw her open a railway timetable and run her fingers down the columns; then she seemed absorbed in some calculation, brow puckered and face upturned. Not yet powdered, a meagre twist of hair at the back of her head, double chin, and raddled neck, she was exposing herself rashly to the unseen observer.

She moved away from the window, and, taking her cheque-book

from a drawer, wrote and tore out several cheques. Then she put a pair of white pyjamas at the foot of the bed, and silently left the room.

Alone, Chéri took several deep breaths, realizing that he had hardly dared to breathe since Léa had left the bed. He got up, put on the pyjamas, and opened a window. 'It's stifling in here,' he gasped. He had the vague uncomfortable feeling of having done something reprehensible. 'Because I pretended to be asleep? But I've watched Léa a hundred times just after she's got out of bed. Only, this time, I made the pretence of being asleep.'

The dazzling light restored the rose-pink glow of the room, and the delicate nacreous tints of the picture by Chaplin smiled down at him from the wall. Chéri bowed his head and shut his eyes, in an effort to remember the room as it had looked the night before – the mysterious colour, like the inside of a water-melon, the enchanted dome of lamplight, and, above all, his exaltation when reeling under the intensity of his pleasures.

'You're up! The chocolate's already on its way.'

He was pleased to note that it had taken Léa only these few moments to do her hair, touch up her face, and spray herself with the familiar scent. The room seemed suddenly to be filled with the cheerful sound of her lovely voice, and with the smell of chocolate and hot toast. Chéri sat down beside the two steaming cups and was handed the thickly buttered toast by Léa. She did not suspect that he was trying to find something to say, for she knew that he was seldom talkative, especially when he was eating. She enjoyed a good breakfast, eating with the haste and preoccupied gaiety of a woman who, her trunks packed, is ready to catch her train.

'Your second piece of toast, Chéri?'

'No, thank you, Nounoune.'

'Not hungry any more?'

'Not hungry.'

With a smile, she shook her finger at him. 'You know what you're in for! You're going to swallow down two rhubarb pills!'

He wrinkled his nose, shocked. 'Listen, Nounoune. You've got a mania for fussing ...'

'Ta ti ta ta! That's my look out. Put out your tongue. You won't show it me! Then wipe off your chocolate moustache, and let's have a quick sensible talk. Tiresome subjects can't be dealt with too quickly!'

She stretched across the table to take Chéri's hand and hold it between her own.

'You've come back. That was our fate. Do you trust yourself to me? I'll be responsible for you.'

She could not help breaking off, and closed her eyes as if hugging her victory. Chéri noticed the flush on his mistress's face.

'Oh!' she continued in a lower voice. 'When I think of all that I never gave you, all that I never said to you! When I think that I believed you merely a passing fancy, like all the others – only a little more precious than all the others! What a fool I was not to understand that you were my love, *the* love, the great love that comes only once!'

When she opened her blue eyes, they seemed to have become bluer, gaining depth in the shade of her eyelids, and her breathing was uneven.

'Oh!' Chéri prayed inwardly. 'Don't let her ask me a question, don't let her expect an answer from me now! I couldn't speak a single word.'

She gave his hand a little shake. 'Come along, let's be serious. As I was saying – we're leaving, we've already left. What will you do about *over there?* Let Charlotte arrange all the settlement details – it's much the wisest – and make her be generous, I beg of you. How will you let them know *over there?* A letter, I imagine. None too easy, but the less ink spilled, the better. We'll see about that between us. Then there's the question of your luggage. I've none of your things here any more. Such little details are far more upsetting than a major decision, but don't worry too much. ... Will you kindly stop tearing the skin off the side of your toe all the time! That's the way to get an ingrowing toe-nail!'

Automatically, he let his foot drop to the floor. Under the weight of his sullen taciturnity, he found it a strain to focus his jaded attention on what Léa was saying. He stared at his mistress's happy, animated, imperious features, and asked himself vaguely: 'Why does she look so happy?'

His bewilderment became so obvious that Léa stopped in the

middle of her monologue on their chances of buying old Berthel-lemy's yacht from him. 'Could anyone believe that you've not got one word of advice to give? Oh, you might still be twelve!'

Chéri, snatched from his stupor, put a hand to his forehead and looked at Léa, his eyes filled with melancholy.

'Being with you, Nounoune, is likely to keep me twelve for half a century.'

She blinked her eyes several times as if he had breathed on their lids, and let silence settle again.

'What are you trying to say?' she asked at last.

'Nothing, except what I did say, Nounoune. Nothing but the truth. And can you deny it, you, the most honest person alive?'

She decided to laugh, but her gaiety masked a terrible fear.

'But half your charm lies in your childishness, stupid! Later on it will be the secret of your eternal youth. Why complain of it? And you have the cheek to complain of it to *me*!'

'Yes, Nounoune. Do you expect me to complain to anyone but you?' and he caught hold of the hand she had taken away. 'My own Nounoune, dearest, darling Nounoune, I'm not only complaining of myself: I'm accusing you!'

She felt the grip of his firm hand. Instead of looking away, his large dark eyes with lashes gleaming clung pitifully to hers. She was determined not to tremble, yet. 'It's nothing, it's nothing,' she thought. 'It calls only for two or three sharp words and he'll become insulting, then sulky, and then I'll forgive him. ... It's no more than that.' But she failed to find the quick rebuke which would change the expression on his face. 'Come, come, child ... You know quite well there are certain jokes I will not tolerate.' But at the same moment she knew her voice to be sounding false and feeble. 'How badly I said that ... bad theatre. ...'

It was half past ten, and the sun was now shining on the table between them. Léa's polished nails twinkled in its beams; but the light fell also on the soft flabby skin on the back of her well-shaped hands and on her wrists. This emphasized – like criss-crossings on a clay soil when heavy rain is followed by a dry spell – the complicated network of tiny concentric grooves and miniature parallelograms. Léa rubbed her hands absent-mindedly, turning her head to make

Chéri look out of the window; but he persisted in his miserable, hang-dog moodiness. The two hands were pretending, as if in disgrace, to toy with a loop of her belt. Brusquely he pounced upon them, kissed and kissed them again, then pressed his cheek against them, murmuring 'My Nounoune. ... Oh, my poor Nounoune ...'

'Let me alone,' she cried with inexplicable anger, snatching her hands away from him.

She took a moment to regain her control, frightened of her weakness, for she had been on the verge of tears. As soon as she was able, she smiled and spoke.

'So now it's me you're sorry for! Why did you accuse me a moment ago?'

'I was wrong,' he said humbly. 'For me you have been always ...' He made a gesture to express his inability to find words worthy of her.

'*You have been?*' she underlined in a biting voice. 'That sounds like an obituary notice, my good child!'

'You see ...' he began reproachfully.

He shook his head, and she saw only too well that she could not rouse any anger in him. She tightened all her muscles, and reined in her thoughts with the help of those few words, ever the same, and inwardly repeated again and again: 'Here he is, in front of my eyes. I've only to look to see he's still there. He's not out of reach. But is he still here, with me, really and truly?'

Her thoughts escaped from the domination of these repeated phrases, only to sink into a great unvoiced lament. 'Oh! if only, if only I could somehow be returned to the moment when I was saying, "Your second piece of toast, Chéri!" for that moment's only just round the corner – it's not yet lost and gone for ever! Let's start again from there. The little that's taken place since won't count – I'll wipe it out, I'll wipe it out. I'm going to talk to him as though we're back where we were a moment ago. I'm going to talk to him about our departure, our luggage.'

She did, in fact, speak, and said, 'I see ... I see I cannot treat as a man a creature who, from sheer feebleness of character, can drive two women to distraction. Do you think that I don't understand? You like your journeys short, don't you? Yesterday at Neuilly, here today, but tomorrow! Tomorrow, where? Here? No, no, my child, no need to lie, that guilty look would never take in even a woman stupider than I am, if there is one like that over there. ...'

She threw out an arm to indicate Neuilly with so violent a gesture that she upset a cake-stand, which Chéri picked up again. Her words had sharpened her grief into anguish, an angry jealous anguish pouring forth like a young wife's outburst. The rouge on her cheek turned to the deep purple of wine-lees; a strand of her hair, crimped by the curling-tongs, wriggled down her neck like a small dry snake.

'And even the woman over there, even your wife won't be found waiting there every time you choose to come back home! A wife, my child, may not always be easy to find, but she's much easier to lose! You'll have yours kept under lock and key by Charlotte, eh? That's a marvellous idea! Oh, how I'll laugh, the day when ...'

Chéri got up, pale and serious. 'Nounoune! ...'

'Why Nounoune? What d'you mean, Nounoune? Do you think you're going to frighten me? You want to lead your own life, do you? Go ahead! You're bound to see some pretty scenes, with a daughter of Marie-Laure's. She may have thin arms and a flat behind, but that won't prevent her from ...'

'I forbid you, Nounoune!'

He seized her by the arm; but she rose, vigorously shook herself free, and broke into hoarse laughter: 'Why, of course, "I forbid you to say a word against my wife!" Isn't that it?'

He walked round the table, trembling with indignation, and went straight up to her. 'No, I forbid you – d'you hear me? – I forbid you to spoil my Nounoune!' She retreated to the end of the room, babbling, 'What's that? what's that?' He followed her as though bent on chastising her. 'You heard what I said. Is that the way for Nounoune to speak? What do you mean by such behaviour? Cheap little jibes like Madame Peloux's, is that what you go in for? To think they could come from you, Nounoune, from you. ...'

Arrogantly he threw back his head. 'I know how Nounoune should speak. I know how she ought to think. I've had time to learn. I've not forgotten the day when you said to me, just before I married, "At least don't be cruel. Try not to make her suffer. I have the feeling

116

that a doe is being thrown to a greyhound." Those were your words. That's really you. And the night before I married, when I ran away to come and see you, I remember you said to me ...'

He could not go on, but all his features were bright with the memory.

'Darling, pull yourself together.' He put his hands on Léa's shoulders. 'And even last night,' he went on, 'it wasn't the first time you asked me whether I might not have hurt somebody *over there*! My Nounoune, I knew you as a fine woman, and I loved you as a fine woman, when we first started. If we have to make an end of it, must you start behaving like all the other women?'

She dimly felt the cunning behind the compliment and sat down, hiding her face in her hands.

'How hard you are, how hard,' she stammered. 'Why did you come back? ... I was so calm on my own, getting so used to ...'

She heard herself lying and stopped.

'Well, *I* wasn't!' Chéri said quickly. 'I came back because ... because ...'

He raised his arms, let them drop, and lifted them again. 'Because I couldn't go on without you, there's no point in looking for any other explanation.'

For a moment no word was spoken.

Quite overcome, she looked at this impatient young man, who with light feet and open arms, as white as a seagull, seemed poised for flight.

Chéri let his dark eyes rove all over her body.

'Oh, you can be proud of yourself,' he said suddenly. 'You can be proud of yourself for having made me – and what's more for three months – lead such a life, such a life!'

'I did?'

'Who else, if it wasn't you? If a door opened, it was Nounoune; the telephone rang, Nounoune; a letter in the garden postbox, perhaps Nounoune. ... In the very wine I drank, I looked for you, and I never found a Pommery to equal yours. And then at nights ... Oh, heavens above!'

He was walking up and down the carpet with rapid, noiseless steps. 'I know now what it is to suffer for a woman, and no mistake!

After you, I know what all the other women will be ... dust and ashes! Oh, how well you've poisoned me!'

She drew herself up slowly in her chair, and, letting her body turn now this way, now that, followed Chéri's movements. Her cheeks were dry, rather shiny, and their fevered flush made the blue of her eyes almost intolerable. He was walking up and down, head lowered, and he never stopped talking.

'Imagine Neuilly with you not there, the first days after my return! For that matter, everything – with you not there! I almost went mad. One night, the child was ill – I no longer remember what it was, headache, pains, something. I felt sorry for her, but I had to leave the room; otherwise nothing in the world could have stopped me saying, "Wait, don't cry, I'll go and fetch Nounoune and she'll make you well" – and you would have come, wouldn't you, Nounoune? Great heavens, what a life it was. ... I took on Desmond at the Hôtel Morris, paid him well into the bargain, and sometimes at night I would tell him stories. ... I used to speak as if you were unknown to him. "Old boy, there's never been a skin like hers. ... Take one look at that cabochon sapphire of yours, and then hide it away for ever, because no light can turn the blue of *her* eyes to grey!" I used to tell him how you could be tough when you wanted to be; and that no one had ever got the better of you, least of all me! I used to say, "That woman, old boy, when she's wearing just the right hat" – the dark blue one with the white wing, Nounoune, last summer's – "and with the way she has of putting on her clothes – you can match her against any other woman you may choose – and she'll put every one of them in the shade!" And then that wonderful manner you have of walking – of talking – your smile – the erect way you hold yourself, I used to say to him – to Desmond: "Ah! A woman like Léa *is* something!" '

He snapped his fingers with proprietary pride and stopped, quite out of breath from his talking and walking. 'I never said all that to Desmond,' he thought, 'and yet I'm not telling lies. Desmond understood all right.'

He wanted to go on and glanced at Léa. She was still ready to listen. Sitting bolt upright now, she exposed to him in the full light her noble face in its disarray, the skin shining like wax where the hot tears had dried. Her cheeks and chin were pulled down by an invisible weight, and this added a look of sadness to the trembling corners of her mouth. Chéri found intact amidst this wreckage of beauty the lovely commanding nose and the eyes as blue as a blue flower.

'And so you see, Nounoune, after months of that sort of life, I come back here, and ...' He pulled himself up, frightened by what he had nearly said.

'You come back here, and find an old woman,' Léa said calmly, in a whisper.

'Nounoune! Listen, Nounoune!'

He threw himself on his knees beside her, looking like a guilty, tongue-tied child no longer able to hide his misdemeanour.

'And you find an old woman,' Léa repeated. 'So what are you afraid of, child?'

She put her arms round his shoulders, and felt his body rigid and resistant, in sympathy with the hurt she was suffering. 'Come, cheer up, my Chéri. Don't cry, my pretty. ... What is it you're afraid of? Of having hurt me? Far from it: I feel so grateful to you.'

He gave a sob of protestation, finding no strength to gainsay her.

She put her cheek against his tousled black hair. 'Did you say all that, did you really think all that of me? Was I really so lovely in your eyes, tell me? And so kind? At the age when a woman's life is so often over, was I really the loveliest for you, the most kind, and were you really in love with me? How grateful I am to you, my darling! The finest, did you say? ... My poor child.'

He let himself go, while she supported him in her arms.

'Had I really been the finest, I should have made a man of you, and not thought only of the pleasures of your body, and my own happiness. The finest! Oh, no, my darling, I certainly wasn't that, since I kept you to myself. And now it's almost too late. ...'

He seemed to be asleep in Léa's arms; but his obstinately tight-shut eyelids quivered incessantly, and with one lifeless hand he was clutching hold of her négligée and slowly tearing it.

'It's almost too late, it's almost too late. But all the same ...' She leaned over him. 'Listen to me, my darling. Wake up, my pretty, and listen to me with your eyes open. Don't be afraid of looking at me. I am, after all, the woman you were in love with, you know, the finest woman ...'

119

He opened his eyes, and his first tearful glance was already filled with a selfish, mendicant hope.

Léa turned away her head. 'His eyes ... Oh, we must get this over quickly. ...' She put her cheek against his forehead.

'It was I, child, it was my real self who said to you, "Don't cause unnecessary pain; spare the doe. ..." I had quite forgotten, but luckily you remembered. You are breaking away from me very late in the day, my naughty little boy; I've been carrying you next to my heart for too long, and now you have a load of your own to carry: a young wife, perhaps a child. ... I am to blame for everything you lack. ... Yes, yes, my pretty, here you are, thanks to me, at twenty-five, so light-hearted, so spoilt, and at the same time so sad. ... I'm very worried about you. You're going to suffer and make others suffer. You who have loved me. ...'

His fingers tightened their grip on her négligée, and Léa felt the sharp nails of her 'naughty child' bite into her breast.

'You who have loved me,' she went on after a pause, 'will you be able to? ... I don't know how to explain what I mean. ...'

He drew back in order to listen: and she could barely restrain herself from saying, 'Put your hand back on my breast and your nails where they have left their mark; my strength abandons me as soon as your flesh is parted from mine.' Instead, she leaned over him as he knelt in front of her, and continued: 'You have loved me, and you will regret ...'

She smiled at him, looking down into his eyes.

'What vanity, eh! ... But you will regret me! I beg of you, when you're tempted to terrify the girl entrusted to your care and keeping, do restrain yourself! At such moments, you must find for yourself the wisdom and kindness you never learned from me. I never spoke to you of the future. Forgive me, Chéri – I've loved you as if we were both destined to die within the same hour. Because I was born twenty-four years before you, I was doomed, and I dragged you down with me. ...'

He was listening very attentively, which made his face look hard. She put her hand on his forehead to smooth the furrows of anxiety.

'Can you see us, Chéri, going out to lunch together at Armenonville! ... Can you see us inviting Monsieur and Madame Lili! ...'

She gave a sad little laugh, and shivered.

'Oh, I'm just about as done for as that old creature. ... Quick, quick, child, run off after your youth! Only a small piece of it has been snipped off by ageing women: all the rest is there for you and the girl who is waiting for you. You've now had a taste of youth! It never satisfies, but one always goes back for more. Oh, you had started to make comparisons before last night. ... And what am I up to now, doling out all this advice and displaying the greatness of my soul! What do I know of you two? She loves you: it's her turn to tremble; but her misery will come from passion and not from perverted mother-love. And you will talk to her like a master, not capriciously, like a gigolo. Quick, quick, run off. ...'

She spoke in tones of hasty supplication. He listened, standing planted before her, his chest bare, his hair tempestuous: and so alluring, that she had to clasp her hands to prevent their seizing hold of him. He guessed this, perhaps, and did not move away. For an instant they shared a lunatic hope – do people feel like this in mid-air when falling from a tower? – then the hope vanished.

'Go,' she said in a low voice. 'I love you. It's too late. Go away. But go away at once. Get dressed!'

She rose and fetched him his shoes, spread out his crumpled shirt and his socks. He stood helpless, moving his fingers awkwardly as if they were numb. She had to find his braces and his tie; but she was careful not to go too close to him and offered him no further help. While he was dressing, she glanced into the courtyard several times, as if she were expecting a carriage at the door.

He looked even paler when he was dressed, and a halo of fatigue round his eyes made them seem larger.

'You don't feel ill?' she asked him. And she added timidly, lowering her eyes, 'You could always lie down for a little.' But at once she pulled herself together and came over to him, as though he were in great danger. 'No, no, you'll be better at home. Hurry, it's not yet midday; a good hot bath will soon put you to rights, and then the fresh air ... Here are your gloves. ... Your hat? On the floor, of course. Put your coat on, there's a nip in the air. Au revoir, my Chéri, au revoir. That's right. And tell Charlotte that ...' She closed the door behind him, and silence put an end to her vain and desperate words. She heard Chéri stumble on the staircase and she ran to the window. He was going down the front steps and then he stopped in the middle of the courtyard.

'He's coming back! He's coming back!' she cried, raising her arms.

An old woman, out of breath, repeated her movements in the long pier-glass, and Léa wondered what she could have in common with that crazy creature.

Chéri continued on his way towards the street. On the pavement he buttoned up his overcoat to hide his crumpled shirt. Léa let the curtain fall back into place; but already she had seen Chéri throw back his head, look up at the spring sky and the chestnut trees in flower, and fill his lungs with the fresh air, like a man escaping from prison.